CAIRO

SURRENDER

www.barbarianspy.com

This book is copyright © habu 2010
Published by BarbarianSpy in 2011.
Cover design by S Bush © 2011
Cover Photo © Francesco Cura | Dreamstime.com

ISBN: 978-1-921879-70-8

Published by BarbarianSpy, an imprint of Cyberworld Publishing
Jindalee St, Toronto, Australia

Barbarian Spy
for Literary Heat

BOOKS BY DIRK HESSIAN
Blue and Gray
Colonel's Treasure
Beginning of Time
Prophecy of Noto
The King's Men
Labyrinth
BOOKS BY HABU
The Indian Prince
The Handyman
Grab Bag
Cairo Surrender
Fetish Galore!
Homeward Bound
Journey to Mirage
Choke Hold
Sporting Life
BOOKS BY SHABBU
Dirty Pool
Operation Black Jade
Yap, Yap
Cigars!
Angel in the Barn
Gayly Complicated
Despoiling David
The Tree of Idleness
Rough Road to Happiness
I Met a Man
The Interview
Rough Road to Happiness
BOOKS BY SABB
The Legend of Holleystone Grange
Surprise Encounters

CAIRO

SURRENDER

BY

HABU

CHAPTER ONE: CAIRO CHAOS

The times were such that it was folly for anyone of European visage to walk the avenues and alleys of Cairo alone. It had been four years of fear and chaos in Cairo capped by the assassination in the city in November, 1924, of the British governor general of Sudan, Sir Lee Stack. The city was caught in the vice of the British pressuring the Egyptian king to bow to the client state demands of British foreign policy needs and the upstart Wafd party in Egypt pressing to end British influence altogether.

Viscount Edmund Allenby, British high commissioner for Egypt and Sudan and sponsor of the creation of a sovereign Egypt, was taking a hard line, demanding that Egypt apologize, prosecute the assassins, and pay a crippling indemnity. The Wafd was taking an even harder line, sending bandits out into the streets to assail and kidnap for exorbitant ransom any European or British sympathizer it could lay its hands on.

In response, the foreign community, in its arrogance and confidence, did what it always did—it donned its suffocating, tight-fitting costumes of the latest style in Europe, completely ignoring the demands for cooler wear of the Egyptian deserts, and it went to Shepheard's for dinner and to see and be seen in sophisticated and oblivious London splendor.

For its part Shepheard's Hotel, occupying a commanding spot in Cairo near the banks of the Nile, was doing what it did best—perpetuating a life of European opulence as it had done for the past eighty years, without a thought to the tension and forming revolution in the street.

On this night, the hotel was in full cry, its rooms fully booked by those coming and going—archaeologists in abundance following the opening of the tomb of the boy pharaoh, Tutankhamun, in the Theban hills of the Valley of the Kings a mere two years previously; the families of British military officers meeting their sons, fathers, and husbands on furlough down from action in the uprisings in Sudan; and the occasional inveterate wealthy European and American tourist in search of adventure and danger and the right to say they were there first. Its public dining and party rooms were overflowing with revelers grasping for the glories and privileges of yesteryear and trying to shut out the cries for change and independence from the Egyptian street.

And down a long, not easily found corridor at the rear of the hotel, the men of power and position in Egypt moved to and from a special dining room not marked on any public sketch of the hotel: the Gentlemen's Dining Room. Here no skirt was seen or swished. No man of only middling import was permitted entrance. Here among the stark white, starched tablecloths and napkins, the gold-rimmed china, the solid-silver plate, and a blue haze of smoke rising to the pinnacle of the coffered roof above a square room, centered by a three-tiered bubbling fountain, dining galleries bordering a central area, and stained-glass clerestory windows on three walls, dined the brains, financial backbone, literary heart, and military muscle of the British empire presence in the Mediterranean and northern Africa.

Dining that evening, on the western balcony tier—being denied access to the ground-floor, central hall by his ethnic origin even though his position both as a political and financial force and a literary light was supreme—was Pasha Rushdy Abazar, scion of a family that traced its origins back to Abraham's tent and that had traded ruling status in Egypt off with only two other families for the past two centuries.

Abazar was listening to his dining companion, the minister of culture in the current regime—and, not incidentally, his cousin—while trying his best not to draw the attention of those throughout the dining room—and particularly those Europeans permitted in the dining area below. Abazar was somewhat of a recluse, but his books—

many considered a bit racy and suggestive—well, more than a bit—were all the rage throughout the British colonial empire at the moment.

He was a man of mystery—fabulously wealthy, average sized but quite well-built of stature, powerfully connected to all factions in Egypt, cerebral, sharp-tongued, and bigger-than-life darkly handsome. When the British social scientists argued that the Arab could come close to becoming civilized, it was Abazar they were imaging.

Many of those below would have loved to invite Abazar to descend the social division of the stairs from the balcony seating to the main floor and join them both to break the tedium of the severely limiting, constantly repetitive small talk of their never-changing dinner companions and to be titillated by trying to discover through guarded discussion if half of the nefarious activities attributed to Abazar and alluded to in his writings were true.

For his part, Abazar would have enjoyed descending that staircase just to see and enjoy the shock waves that would reverberate through the stagnant society that was the British expatriate community of Cairo.

As Abazar listened to his cousin drone on with half an ear, received messages and gave instructions to a flunkey lurking near the table at frequent intervals, and watched what passed as the cream of the European community in Egypt below watch him and speculate on what he was thinking, his attention was arrested by a flurry of activity at the central door to the lower dining area and the near-simultaneous craning of heads on the ground floor to this entry.

So staid was the privileged foreign community here that Abazar, even as rarely as he dined here, could close his eyes and identify exactly where everyone below was sitting— because that's where they always sat, much like people do in their houses of worship. The Gentlemen's Dining Room was, in essence, such a house of worship.

On this night nearly every chair was filled—with the exception of the table of the club steward, Sir Hilary Wainsworth-Jones, which sat empty, as well it should, because Sir Hilary was deeper down into the continent climbing Mount Kilimanjaro.

Abazar held his breath, as did everyone at the tables below, and trained his eyes to the room's main entrance, as did everyone in the room except for his inattentive, babbling cousin, as two men glided into the room, and, walking behind a proud, strutting maître d', were ushered to the club steward's table. The table was located next to the fountain, almost in the center of the room—and on a dais above the floor level, so that it could be seen from any vantage point in the dining room. Headwaiters in black tails and white gloves rushed forward and pulled chairs, faces reverently lowered, as

11

the two men—intriguingly, men of unknown origin and import—settled in their own gilded thrones, and, for a brief moment the two were lost to view by a bevy of table waiters in black pants and starched white shirts and also wearing immaculate white gloves who revolved around the two, making them comfortable, filling the wine glass of one, explaining the menu, suggesting specials and particular delicacies, and taking orders.

There was nothing special in visage about the older man. He was tall and florid, strongly built but beginning to lose the battle with corpulence. In other words, he was much like most other men in the hall. He was dressed in a gray pinstripe suit and had solicitor and family retainer written all over his countenance.

Abazar dismissed him immediately, as would have any of the diners below if they were not racking their brains on just who this might be who was not only received in the Gentleman's Dining Room at Shepheard's but who also was welcome at the club steward's table.

Some of the men, including Abazar, were absorbed in scrutinizing the other man. And, like Abazar, they were undressing him and dreaming of all they would love to do with him.

The man was young—barely a man at all. He was white. That was the first image of the young man that struck

Abazar. And it wasn't because he was Caucasian, even though he was. It was rather because he was dressed entirely in stark white and because everything else about him reflected whiteness—even the hint of his innocence. A beautifully cut supper suit that was immaculately white and fit him as only a richly and expensively cut suit could do. But the white wasn't contained to that. His hair, set in curls around his achingly beautiful face, with heavy-lashed sultry eyes and full, pouting lips, was white blond. And his skin was as the milk-creamiest white marble—almost translucent. And the way he lowered his eyes and seemed in awe of his surroundings cried out of a pristine, unwritten slate—virginal. Abazar immediately surmised that he was ill or had been ill—and it made him want to hold the young man and stroke him and tell him everything would be all right, that Abazar would protect him and make everything all right.

But such was the sensuousness and compelling vulnerability of the lean, but perfectly formed—and diminutive, if his dining companion could be judged as anything but a giant in comparison—youth that Abazar's imagining went well beyond the instinct to protect and cradle. He wanted to possess this young man—sexually. He wanted to lay his hand on the young man's marble breast and feel the quickening of the beating of his heart and devour his eyes with his own, watching for the sizzling surrender at the moment of entry of his justifiably proud cock into the young man's passage. Abazar knew that the young man must be virginal—every shred of his demeanor screamed of this. And, as had happened so many times before, Abazar reasoned that he must be the first—as so often he was.

He tore his eyes from the young man—but only with great effort—and scanned the room, where conversation had initially halted completely. But the buzzing of queries and gossip slowly rebuilt while all eyes in the room remained glued on these mysterious interlopers. There was no doubt of the topic of their renewed discussion. And among these men of power and wealth and position, Abazar was able to pick out one here and two there—more than would be imagined—men who were watching the youth as Abazar was. And who wanted to possess him—sexually—as achingly as Abazar did. Abazar knew most of these men—biblically—and he had taken the virginity and initiated "the life" for more of them than he could count on his hands. And more often than not, the gazes of these men went from the youth to the balcony, where Abazar sat, gauging whether Abazar too had taken note and assessing their chances of being the first if Abazar had.

Abazar was a master seducer of men. And whispered about, even within the colonial community, were tales of his prowess and staying power, and, most especially, his

14

endowments—and his ability to convince the virginal to accord him entrance. He knew he was referred to as the Stallion of Heliopolis, Heliopolis being the suburb of Cairo where his family's stronghold palace, its origins traceable back to the pharaohs, was located. The appellation amused Abazar, and he was fond, in the wake of a conquest while his prey was still moaning of being split unto death, of laughing and asking if mere "stallion" did him justice.

"Who is that? Do you know?" he asked abruptly, interrupting his cousin in midsentence on a request to recite poetry at a museum opening in Alexandria.

"Who? What? Where?" the cousin, confused by being put off stride just as he was getting to the crux of why he had invited Abazar to dine here, sputtered.

"Down there. At the steward's table. You must have been the only man in the room who missed their entrance."

"What? Where? Oh, I believe that is Sir Cecil Pills. Solicitor to Allenby, I think. Top drawer. Noble firm, offices in London, on the Continent, and even in America, I think. Some place called Boston. People genuflect as his passage, I understand. There was some sort of scandal. Whisperings of something sordid. The Prince of Wales or something. But it only seemed to add to his stature. Incomprehensible these English. They need to go, the whole lot of—"

The cousin suddenly realized where he was and what he was saying, and his jaw shut with a snap that sounded like the crack of a rifle and caused the turning of heads nearby. He turned ashen and looked as if he might be in need of a bucket—which, in Shepheard's would have been silver with crystal handles and delivered by a ramrod-straight-backed man in livery and white kid gloves.

"Mind your tongue in here, cousin," Abazar said. But he said it with amusement and almost a sense of detachment. This wasn't one of his favorite cousins, and Abazar was trained to go blank at any hint of partisanship. He supported his causes, but it was a family trait to know what and how to balance and to forever land on your feet. Lately, the effort had been taxing, though. Both the British and the Wafd were increasingly demanding palpable displays of loyalties. Abazar felt that it might be time for another prolonged visit to Paris, Rome, and Istanbul. "And I don't mean the old pile in gray," he continued. "Who is the luscious young man with him?"

There was a pause, and then a flustered whisper. "You can't have him, Rushdy. There are men here who not even you can touch."

"I didn't ask for an assessment," Abazar snapped. "I asked for an identification."

"I believe his name is Michael Powell. American. Fabulously wealthy family and he has inherited it all. Coal and railroads, I believe. And large land holdings in England. A portfolio that transcends the continents."

"Inherited it all? How so? He looks like he's barely in his majority."

"I said you can't have him, Abazar. It would be the undoing of all of us. I can see how you look at him. I know you want them barely baked."

"Just answer the question, cousin. How has he come to be so rich and to be here in Egypt?"

"It will do you no good. He came with a phalanx of guardians. I don't know of any visitor as protected and well-connected as—"

Abazar scrunched down at the table, and hissed in his cousin's ear. "I will lay him on his back on the golden table in my study, and slowly peel his clothes from him as he whimpers and begs me in despair for the shaft—begging me for it. And I will lower my face to his nipples and cause him to cry out and then do so again, more plaintively, more pleadingly, as I work my oiled fist into his virginal hole in preparation for my even larger—"

"Please cousin, please, be silent," the cousin hissed in consternation. He was beginning to sweat.

"Then answer my simple question. It is just a question of information. It is no concern of yours why I ask."

"His parents—I believe he was an only child—were killed in an accident on their own railroad, I understand. He was crushed by the event, and his minders have done all they can to amuse him and pull him from his depression. He had expressed interest in the excavation of Tutankhamen's tomb, and he had done no more than mention it before an expedition was launched. The river barge *Isis* has been chartered, and they leave for Karnak on the Nile in the morning. Or so I've heard. I was consulted, I'll admit, about present conditions in Cairo, and I counseled that they embark on the Nile as quickly as possible."

"A pity," Abazar murmured. "Just the night. I believe it would take longer than that."

The cousin relaxed, feeling the crisis was over. Abazar was going to see reason. That was unusual for him. Usually, the stronger the challenge, the more interested he was. When he had taken the young son of the pope the previous spring, he had had to work his way through waves of Swiss guards and literally pull him off the cock of the Austrian prince. But he had done it—and subsequently had enjoyed the Austrian as well—not to mention several of the Swiss guards.

"The gall," Abazar hissed, which caused the cousin to look up sharply. He followed Abazar's gaze and focused on the center of his attention quick enough to see Raymond Little, an assistant of Allenby's, who was functioning as the de facto police chief of the city of Cairo and was using a heavy hand in dealing with all signs of dissent he could put his finger on, appear from somewhere in the swirl of diners and approach the steward's table.

The cousin looked on in horror as he listened to Abazar's heavy breathing and watched the man in gray and youth in white rise and shake hands with Little. At a gesture from the gray-suited man, the police chief sat down at the table. Immediately behind him stood a Nubian in the uniform of the Egyptian police, a veritable mountain of solid muscle of a man. The cousin knew that Little's life was in constant danger, and he wasn't surprised that he kept an intimidating guard at his elbow at all times.

The presence of the Nubian in this position was no more threatening to the social standards than were the army of Egyptian and Sudanese waiters working the room. All were virtually invisible to those who were there to dine—and to be served properly as they had been at Shepheard's for eighty years. They weren't there to dine, so they were invisible—in ways that Abazar and his ilk on the balcony weren't. The existence and necessity of Abazar and his class of Egyptians was recognized and accepted—they were just kept in their place.

"The Prick," Abazar growled. "Always the opportunist."

The cousin almost swallowed his tongue, knowing the ways of Abazar as he did. He might have at least chuckled at the absurdity of what his cousin had said, if he didn't know what was at stake here. Little was as corrupt as they came in Egypt, which was saying much, and was a notorious user of man flesh, the younger and more tender the better, ones whose mark of cruelty when he was done with them would clearly be understood as his work. He preferred young Egyptian men, effeminate ones—dancers usually—ones who would not be missed or remarked on if they suddenly disappeared after an overindulgent night. But the cousin could see that the youth in white was so exotic that Little could easily be aroused by him.

Although Abazar was trembling with emotion beside him, the cousin saw this as a relief. Abazar would have to bow to the inevitable and let this one pass. The challenge was just too great. Little had gotten there first. A chill went up the cousin's spine at the thought of the danger he knew the youth was in—and he muttered a little prayer to Allah that the expedition set off before Little realized how limited his opportunity was.

His attention was snapped back to reality, though, when Abazar called his flunky over and whispered in his ear. The cousin watched in building terror as the message was conveyed through a chain of increasingly senior waiters until the maître d' was at the shoulder of the man in gray at the steward's table.

The man looked up at the balcony and then whispered to the maître d', and the diners—ever in tune with any shifting of the routine—held their knives and forks in abeyance as the message transited back up the social barrier of the staircase, and the head waiter of the balcony leaned down and whispered a message to Abazar.

Everyone in the room could read the message in Abazar's frozen reception.

"I'm sorry, Pasha Rushdy Abazar," the waiter intoned with trembling voice, "but Sir Cecil says it would not be convenient for them to join you in the smoking room following supper. He says his ward is weary and they must embark on the *Isis* for an early start in the morning."

"Thank you," Abazar responded in an icy tone that made the head waiter's knees begin to buckle. "Do they know who I am?"

"Yes, Pasha. That was made quite clear to them. But they aren't from—"

"Please offer my appreciation for the consideration of the invitation and provide them a bottle of your best champagne as a token of my regard."

Bowing and scraping, the waiter hurried off to do Abazar's bidding, grateful for the opportunity to provide the service—and even more grateful for the excuse not to be on the balcony as Abazar seethed.

For the next half hour, Abazar sat, sinking ever deeper into his chair and into a dark anger, not listening to his cousin, who was doing everything he could to distract the focus of Abazar's attention. Abazar's attention was focused on the silver bucket stand close behind the side of the man in the gray suit, as waiter after waiter tried to fill his glass from the champagne bottle couched in the bucket—and was repeatedly rebuffed so that not a drop of champagne was being consumed. At no time did the man in gray look up at the balcony. The youth in white did scan the room and linger his gaze at the balcony from time to time, but Abazar didn't see that. His attention was plastered to the sliver ice bucket and the rejected champagne bottle.

At the end of the half hour, announcing his movement by a deep rumble from within, Abazar abruptly stood, sending china and silver and crystal scattering across his table and onto the floor. An army of waiters descended on the table to chase the errant implements, dab at the stains on Abazar's black silk evening suit, and apologize abjectly for sins they had not committed.

Abazar was flushed with anger, standing straight and majestically, looking like a god of wrath. The movement did not go unnoticed by anyone in the dining room—anyone but the gray-suited solicitor and the white-suited youth, that is. Indeed, every eye had been surreptitiously watching Abazar since the delivery of the first invitation, and all lips were being moistened with tongues in anticipation of his reaction to the refusal of his gift. Raymond Little seemed to look especially amused by the little drama playing out right under his nose.

This simply was not done in the Gentlemen's Dining Room of the Shepheard's Hotel. None of the men in their lifetime could remember such an instance—and memories had to be searched for any inkling of precedent, which seemed to be couched in tales of sunrise duels on the broad lawn between the hotel and the Nile and tragic, surreptitious funerals.

"Cousin, please. They are looking," the cultural minister croaked in a strangled voice. He reached out to tug at Abazar's sleeve, but his hand was roughly brushed away.

"I will go now," Abazar said in a menacing tone. He snapped his fingers, and his flunky appeared at his side. Whispered instructions were given, and the flunky disappeared into the shadows.

"But we cannot go yet, cousin," the minister hissed. "I told the guards to come back at eleven. We cannot go without guards. You know the streets. We cannot. It's not safe. You've had threats. So I have I. We must wait for—"

"You may wait, as you wish, cousin. I will not."

And then Abazar was on the move. And accompanied by a rising gasp from the diners from one wall to the other, he slowly, and with iron-rod-straight back, descended the stairs from the balcony rather than leaving via the balcony door into the hotel proper. Each and every diner felt the lash of the snapping of the taboo of the staircase, as, with an "I dare anyone" glare and a carriage of righteous indignation, Abazar slowly descended the stairs and departed, head held high—by the main door.

You could have heard a pin drop. For a full five minutes. And then the buzzing started. The buzzing of a hundred hives.

Through it all, the man in gray sat, facing away from the main door, muttering instructions to his ward, who was peeping surreptitiously under charcoal lashes toward the door—seeing the majestic progress of the imposing figure of the Egyptian man without having an iota of an inkling what was causing all of the tension—but somehow drawn to the man who was causing all of the commotion.

When the door to the main dining floor had clicked shut and two headwaiters belatedly positioned themselves in front of the closed panels, the man in gray motioned to a waiter and, as the buzzing gained strength, he watched his glass and that of the city's police chief being filled with champagne from the iced bottle in the silver bucket at his elbow, and then he saluted the police chief and tossed off the champagne. A waiter was immediately at his elbow to refill his glass.

Within hours the foreign community was abuzz with reports of what the nearest diners heard the man in gray then say.

"I've heard that conditions had become lax out here—Allenby told me that—but I had no idea they were now letting natives in the lobby of Shepheard's, let alone in the Gentleman's Dining Room. What is the world coming to, one wonders."

CHAPTER TWO: RAWEST CAIRO

The dramatic departure of Pasha Rushdy Abazar took all of the fizz out of the evening in the Gentlemen's Dining Room at Shepheard's. Nothing was going to happen that evening to top that, and many of the gentlemen were suddenly remembering forgotten engagements and bustling off to start spreading the word of the latest affront on civilization inflicted at the very center of proper society.

Those at the steward's table also rose soon thereafter, Sir Cecil and Raymond Little adjourning to the men's smoking lounge for a cigar, brandy, and some private words, with the young man, Michael Powell, being sent off under the protection of the Nubian policeman to finish his studies for the day in one of the receiving rooms off the main lobby before Sir Cecil was ready for them to ascend to their rooms at Shepheard's.

The receiving room was deserted of anyone other than Michael and his guard as Michael sat at a writing desk and poured over the textbook on Egyptian history Sir Cecil was requiring him to read in preparation for the trip up the

Nile to the Valley of the Kings. Sir Cecil was a strict taskmaster when it came to Michael's studies. He was endeavoring to give the man a classic university education without the benefit of a university faculty. Michael had always been held in seclusion by his family as being sensitive, delicate, and prone to illnesses, and Sir Cecil, while striving to educate Michael for the responsibilities of an industrialist in his adulthood, was keeping with the regimen originally set by the parents.

No one bothered to consult Michael on what he wanted to do in life. The family fortune and his inheritance was largely through his mother, who had been British, and thus was mostly located in England and so tied up in stipulations until he reached the age of twenty-five that he was as encumbered by the wishes and desires of Sir Cecil, his guardian, as he had been by his smothering parents. And Sir Cecil told him he had his hands full with keeping the hands of Michael's grasping uncles and aunts and cousins from wheedling big chunks of the estate from Michael's hands even before he could gain control over it—and his life.

Michael wasn't interested in becoming a coal and railroad tycoon. All of this study Sir Cecil forced on him was boring to Michael, and he only did it because Sir Cecil was a tyrant and could be an even worse one when his wishes weren't being attended. This trip, even, was more a function of Sir Cecil's interests than his. Michael cared nothing for dead things—for this boy pharaoh, Tut, who was said to have died young and perhaps under suspicious circumstances. Michael cared more about the living—and he wondered when he would be permitted to live, to feel, to experience. He wasn't even sure what was out there to experience, and although there were ideas and urges that moved him, Sir Cecil was the last one he wanted to discuss these with.

The idea of Egypt didn't repel him. It wasn't that, and he was perfectly happy to be taking this adventure. But it wasn't the dead things of archaeology that attracted him. It was the Romance of the place, the dashing, swarthy men in the flowing tunics they wore and he'd read about in his novels—their sparkling white dishdashas—although it had been a disappointment to him to thus far see the Egyptian men stiffly wearing the same suffocating European dress as he did. Like that man in the dining room, the one who was the focus of so much attention. He was handsome and mysterious looking—and dashing as well. Michael wondered what he would look like in a dishdasha.

To Michael, Egypt and all of the Near East was the romance and dashing adventure that he had found in those novels he had read before Sir Cecil discovered he had them and confiscated them. Michael's favorite had been one entitled *The Prince of the Sands*, which Michael had found fascinating and was just discovering to be titillating as well when Sir Cecil found him with it and took it from him.

Where was that Egypt, Michael wondered.

A waiter came in and moved a porcelain cup of tea from a tray and placed it on the desk beside the book on archaeology Michael was unsuccessfully trying to focus on. Watching Michael carefully to see his preferences, the waiter, a young man not much older than Michael, slender and willowy and of dusky complexion and flashing black eyes, expertly dealt out sugar cubes and poured cream until Michael signaled he was satisfied. But Michael wasn't really satisfied. He couldn't understand why he couldn't be in the smoking room, enjoying a cigar and brandy just as Sir Cecil and that pudgy, drab-looking policeman were doing. Why was he still, at nearly twenty—well nearly nineteen, at least—being treated like a child? What was wealth and position—and youth—worth if they could not be spent.

Michael heard a moaning noise in the corner of the room, and he looked around to find that the Nubian guard had the waiter trapped in a corner and was fondling him and whispering to him in insistent tones. The waiter looked frightened out of his senses and completely out of his depth in how to respond to these advances. Michael looked over to the door out into the lobby to see that it was shut—and very possibly locked. The three of them were alone in the room.

Michael gauged the distance between himself and the door, but he could see in an instant that the Nubian would make it there before he did if he made a sudden move in that direction.

What could he do but pretend that it wasn't happening. That was what his life had been about to now—ignoring the world around him; pretending that nothing untoward was happening. He remembered a remark that Sir Cecil had made earlier in the day—about the chaos that was about in Cairo and further abroad in Egypt now. Of how the military and police had become an all-encompassing and unfettered power unto themselves in combination with the increasing violence in the Cairo streets—that the two of them needed to be wary and as inconspicuous as possible as they passed through on their journey. Sir Cecil had made an explicit point that Michael, in his lithe, youthful blondness, could not possibly be inconspicuous here, so that he was to remain glued to Shepheard's and out of the limelight until they could embark on the *Isis*.

Michael turned his head away, ashamed that he was interested in watching, that within the wave of fright there was a drop of inexplicable arousal that he was too protected, too virginal to begin to fathom, and knowing that this was sinful and was something that Sir Cecil admonished him about incessantly, telling him that he must accept that his visage was such as to be attractive to a certain kind of man and that he needed to protect himself at all costs. A shudder ran through him at the thought of what this ebony monster might do to him if he made any move to intervene—or even to acknowledge that anything was happening in the corner of the room.

He rose and moved over to the French windows that overlooked the stone terrace and gardens of one of the several courtyards that made up the complex of the rambling Shepheard's edifice. He would not look at what was transpiring in the corner, although he tuned his ears to the heavy breathing and moaning and groans he could hear. He had no control over the Nubian. Indeed, the man was so massive and menacing that he frightened Michael.

He would concentrate on looking out into the night, to see what he could pick out as the form of the courtyard garden.

As Michael's eyes became adjusted to the dark, he saw that there was a figure out there. An old crone of an Egyptian woman in a black, swirling garment and a veil. She was pushing a cart filled with who knows what—and she was looking at Michael in the window, where he stood, backlit by the array of candles flickering in the receiving room.

As Michael watched, she unhooked her veil and showed him a broad smile that was missing only a few teeth.

She may have been a beauty at some point in her life, but she was far beyond that point now. But hers was a friendly, benign look.

She beckoned to him and slowly waved her arm across the top of her cart, signaling that she had wares to show him, souvenirs of Egypt that he surely would want.

And Michael was interested.

He also, against his will, was interested in what was happening in the corner of the room, as well. He was confused—and titillated—by the incongruity of it. A raw, rough, sexual act—yes, he had to acknowledge that he knew it was a sexual act—being conducted in a luxuriously appointed anteroom at the very center of proper civilization—with men and women of reserve and breeding sipping their tea just on the other side of the locked door.

At a sharp cry, he looked around, into the corner. There would be no denying now what was happening there. The waiter's legs were off the ground, hooked on the Nubian's hips—and bare, his trousers on the floor at his feet—entangled with those of the Nubian. The waiter's flashing black eyes, overflowing with surprise and pain-pleasure and pleading, were glued to Michael, as if there were some hope of release there. His back was being slid up and down on the scarlet brocade covering the wall, and his dusky brown buttock cheeks were being palmed and squeezed and separated by the Nubian's massive black hands. The Nubian's globular buttocks shimmered and bounced as they rhythmically moved back and forth, back and forth, eliciting a groan and a squeak from the mouth of the waiter with each forward thrust.

The crone was at the window now, offering a stone statuette in her raised hand, smiling hopefully at Michael—wanting something from him just as the beleaguered waiter wanted something from him.

What would the Nubian do when he was finished with the waiter was the thought flashing across Michael's face? Would he dare? Surely it would mean death for him to do anything to Michael here in the luxuriously appointed, protective arms of Shepheard's Hotel. But could the Nubian stop himself now that he'd gone this far? Michael knew nothing of the balance of power in Egypt—who could get away with what.

Drumming in his head was the instruction from Sir Cecil to make himself as wallpaper—cause no ripples, take no chances—while they were in the raw wound that was present-day Cairo.

Michael reached for the latch of the French door and found it was open. He was out into the open air even before he could think of what he'd do next. Just beyond the light cast from the room through the French windows, he stopped and looked around, expecting pursuit. But the Nubian was obviously lost in his current taking—at least for the moment.

Where was the entrance to the hotel proper, Michael wondered. It didn't appear to be off to the side. This courtyard must be on the opposite side of the hotel's façade, he thought. He took a step in one direction and then turned, uncertain, and took a step in another direction.

He felt a hand on his sleeve and whirled around, expecting the Nubian, but finding the crone—still proffering the stone statuette in her upraised hand, smiling her gap-toothed smile.

Michael shrugged, trying to convey that he had no money—Sir Cecil carried any money they spent. And he conveyed as best he could that he was looking for the front entrance to the hotel.

The crone smiled a knowing smile, grasped his sleeve and started guiding him toward the shadows, which appeared to him to be an isolated corner of the courtyard with no passage beyond. He was about to turn from this direction, despite her insistence, when all he could see was a swirl of dirty-white dishdashas below mean, swarthy faces of rough men of the Cairo street. And then a cloth was forced over his head, his wrists and ankles were tied together, and he saw nothing and felt himself lifted from the ground and roughly manhandled across the stone of the terrace.

Michael initially was so shocked by what was happening that he froze. Half way across the terrace, though, the wind was knocked out of him as he was dropped abruptly to the paving stones and heard the sound of a near-silent struggle going around him to the sounds of huffs and groans and short, cut-off muffled cries. He was being trampled under a dozen feet—and then only under a few, and then all was silent for a moment.

He expected to be freed then, but this didn't happen. He was lifted again by several hands and was being carried someplace again. He cried out and struggled as best he could. And then briefly the cloth was removed, but only so that another cloth could be brutally wrapped over his face, covering his mouth and making it hard to breath even through his nose. Then a sharp pain to his jaw, followed by . . . nothing.

CHAPTER THREE: THE DARKEST HOUR

When Michael came to, he was still being carried by the hands of more than one ruffian. The dulling of the sensitivity to his eyes told him that they had entered a darkened area—cool, and damp. The contrast with the dry heat of the Cairo streets, even at night, seemed incongruous to him unless, of course, they were somewhere near the banks of the Nile. He was being carried bumpily down stairs that he discerned were stone from the hollow sound of the flapping feet. He heard the sound of rusty metal grating on metal, he was laid, not too gently, down on a hard surface. Hands were pulling at cloth while he was being released from his bindings—and not just the rough cloth covering he'd been swathed in but his white suit and shirt and shoes and socks as well, down to his linen drawers. Nearly last to come off was the cloth over his head, and with a painful jerk, the binding over his mouth was ripped away. His eyes were having difficulty focusing. He felt the air current and the feet flapping of the withdrawing figures—and then the heavy slam of the door and the rasping of a bolt being shot home.

The light was dim, but bright enough that he caught no glimpse of his assailants before his eyes adjusted to the glare.

He found himself in a square stone-walled, stone-floored cell of dimensions of perhaps eighteen by eighteen feet. There was a single horizontal window opening high on the wall opposite the door. The opening was barred, and he could tell that day had broken because a beam of light, thick with dust particles almost too dense to see through, flooded into the room from the window and lit up a narrow cot placed against the wall to his right. His eyes then went immediately to the far corner of the room to the left, where he saw a square indent in the floor with a circular hole toward the back corner. Above this area was suspended a cistern with a heavy rope hanging down. He reasoned at once what the hole was for and also what the cistern was for. You pulled on the rope and the cistern tipped and water cascaded on anyone standing in the indenture. And the hole was large enough for other purposes as well.

Against the wall to the left was a crude wooden table with uneven legs and two squat stools, also with uneven legs. Above the level of the rude furnishings and set at intervals high on the walls all around the chamber were heavy black iron rings from which short chains ending in manacles dangled. Michael shuddered at the realization of what these were and what purpose this chamber must once have served—unless, of course, it still served that purpose.

Michael sat up on the floor, rubbed his chaffed wrists with his hands, and was unsuccessful in stifling a whimper.

"Ah, company. How nice. I was beginning to think I'd have to entertain myself."

Michael's head jerked up, seeking out the seemingly disembodied voice in what he initially had thought was, beyond him, an empty cell. The voice was a musical baritone, rich in texture, a touch of amusement completely out of place in these surroundings. The accent British, but a slight touch of something else too. But refined, carefully modulated.

He peered through the dust particles in the beam of light from the window and barely discerned movement there, from what he now could see was a second cot, set against the wall opposite the door.

The figure stirred, arose, and materialized through the dust particles. It was a man—a familiar man—an Egyptian. Of average stature and perhaps in his thirties, both of which surprised Michael, because the last time he had seen the man, he had appeared bigger than life and older—more mature.

And the last time Michael had seen him, descending the stairs at the Gentlemen's Dining Room at Shepheard's, commanding the attention of all those present, he also had been elegantly dressed in black silk evening clothes.

Now, like Michael, he was stripped down to linen drawers. And now he was more mysterious, more Egyptian, more feral than he had seemed before. He was dusky skinned and had magnificent musculature. Black curly hair—everywhere—from the crown of his head to his tightly clipped beard, down the line of his chest. And then on down, in a wide band running down his clavicle and ribs and flat belly and into the low-slung waistband of his drawers. His legs were hairiest of all. And what came to Michael's mind immediately were the images of satyrs he'd seen in books—so much so that his eyes descended to the man's feet, half expecting to see cloven hooves, but seeing instead long feet with long, plump, sensuous toes.

Michael shuddered and felt warm inside—without knowing why.

"Come, let me help you up," the man said as he moved to Michael.

Michael said nothing; he moaned and reflexively shrank away.

"Come. I won't harm you. We're both in the same pickle it would appear. And . . . don't I know you from somewhere? Have we met?"

"No. I've just arrived in Cairo," Michael said. It started in a croak, but then he realized that he was able to speak without his voice wavering. "I don't know anyone here," Michael continued. "I don't know why I'm here. It must be some sort of mistake."

"Everything in Cairo is a mistake," the man said somewhat wistfully. "But surely I've seen you."

"Last night. At Shepheard's. We were dining in the same room. My name's Michael. Michael Powell. American. I am just passing through. On my way to Karnak. The young pharaoh's tomb, you know. What's his name."

"Tutankhamun, the boy pharaoh," the man said helpfully.

"Yes, that's him," Michael mumbled.

"Come, Mr. American Michael Powell. My name is Rushdy. Come let me help you up. I won't bite—at least not yet."

Michael gave him a sharp look, which Rushdy Abazar answered with a lopsided "I was just kidding" smile. Abazar reached his hand down, and Michael tentatively raised his and Abazar helped him rise to his feet.

"You can have whichever cot you want," Abazar said. "I only beat you in here by about an hour. I don't feel proprietary yet regarding any of these luxurious amenities."

Once again that smile, and Michael gave a tentative smile back, although it was through a haze of forming teardrops.

40

"Where are we? Why are we here? What's going to happen?" Michael had moved to the cot outlined by the beam of sunlight from the window opening high on the wall and collapsed on the thin mattress in despair.

"Such a lot of questions," Abazar said, retreating back to the other cot and sitting down. "I can answer one of them and perhaps make a good guess as to the rest. You have come to Cairo at a bad time, my lad. It's a pity you could not have come a few years ago. It's a glorious place, it really is. I would have enjoyed showing you around."

Abazar's words, given in a calm voice, clearly trying to soothe the young man, remained unremarked, so he continued. "As to where we are. In a prison cell, of course. Not the government's cells, to be sure. This is the virtual lap of luxury when set against those. This one is clean and doesn't smell of rot—at least yet. And as far as a location on earth, I am fairly certain we are somewhere in Heliopolis, a suburb of Cairo, along the Nile."

"How? How do you surmise this?" the youth asked, drawn in by the soothing, rich voice of the satyr, an image he just couldn't get out of his mind and that was assaulting him with mixed sensations of fear and interest.

"Look out of the window, high up on the horizon. What do you see?"

"A tower. Some sort of tower."

"That's a minaret, from which we Muslims are called to prayer. You will probably hear the call yourself soon enough—and then I will prostrate myself on the floor facing Mecca—assuming I can get my bearings and ascertain which direction Mecca is in. And it's not just any minaret. I recognize it. I live in Heliopolis myself. I can see this self same minaret from my home. That's the one answer to your questions I can provide with surety."

"And the others?" Michael asked in a soft voice, almost not wanting to hear the answers.

"Ah, the others. You are American and obviously wealthy—and I might add, achingly young and handsome and blond—although we will not get into that shall we? It's enough that you are American and wealthy. I would surmise that you are here as a matter of convenient snatching. You evidently placed yourself in a position to be kidnapped. No doubt in a few days, your family will have paid a handsome ransom and you will be back in their comforting arms—with luck, not much the worse for wear. Unless, of course. . . .But, as I said, we won't get into negative thinking, shall we?"

Michael shuddered. He was beginning to think of the possibilities. Visions of the Nubian he had avoided only perhaps to fall into worse straits sprang to his mind.

"And you? Why you?"

"Alas, I left Shepheard's a little precipitously last night—without guards. There are other reasons why I would have been taken when vulnerable. These are volatile times in Cairo. And I am a public figure and was dining at the center of the European community here. I perhaps was a bit out of balance last evening on my loyalties. And just a little out of balance now can be fatal. No, no, I wager you'll be out and on your way up the Nile with a story to fascinate your friends back in America within a day or two," Abazar rushed on. "Whereas I may never be seen again, alas."

"How . . . how can you say that so cavalierly?" Michael asked.

"Life is precious, but it also is fleeting," Abazar answered. "Even in our most settled days, we live on the edge here in Egypt. One must be a fatalist about these things—and enjoy life to the fullest as we live it. Haven't you found that to be the case?"

Michael hung his head and was unable to stifle a perceptible sob.

"Have you not lived life to the fullest, my young Michael? You are rich and young and godlike handsome. You have traveled a quarter of the way around the world. There has been adventure, and wonder, and glorious risk in your life, has there not? You have seen the amazing sights on offer and have loved well and often already. Surely you have."

There was silence for a while, and then a muttered. "No sir, no, there hasn't been any of those things in my life. All of my life has been in study and preparing myself . . . preparing to follow in my parents' footsteps."

"What? That certainly sounds dull. Surely there has been love—and exploration. You shake your head. I cannot believe it. Not one as perfectly formed as you—and that blond hair and the face of an angel. Why, I thought America was civilized. Even in Europe you would have been placed in the care of an experienced older woman—or man, if such be your preference—long before now and shown the glories of life between a pair of plump thighs."

"Please. Please, don't. I have not . . ."

"I do apologize," Abazar said in a soft voice. "I do not mean to distress you. Distract you, yes, but not distress you. Let us speak of other matters. But, I do believe I hear footsteps—and the rasping of the bolt on our door. Ah, yes. Trays. We shall be fed. A feast surely."

A lower section of the door opened, and two trays were pushed into the room. The food wasn't straight from the Gentlemen's Dining Room at Shepheard's. But it looked hearty enough.

Abazar reached down and picked up both trays and placed them on the table and gestured to one of the stools.

"Come, my young Michael. We must maintain our strength. We must eat. No? But you must, I insist. Come."

Michael reluctantly rose from the cot and moved over to the table. Abazar was already eating greedily from one of the trays and drinking the lukewarm coffee.

The young man sat on the stool in front of his tray, but he was just looking at the food.

"Come, eat. After our meal, I will spin stories for us to bide our time—and then, in the heat of the day, we can nap. We can sleep the hours away without any fear of being called lazy, of needing to be doing anything else because anyone else wanted us to do it."

"Stories?" Michael asked.

"Yes, yes. You don't know, of course. You couldn't know. But I am a storyteller. Of some renown, even outside Egypt, if I do say so myself. Haven't you read any Egyptian novels? Didn't you do that in preparation for your journey up the Nile? That is the best way to get the sense of a place, you know. Read its literature."

"I did try. I tried reading Egyptian novels. One I did find very interesting. It was one called *The Prince of the Sands*. But my guardian took it away from me. He said it was not something I should be reading—and he wanted me to read only books on archaeology and finance. I find those a bit dull, though."

Abazar smiled and gave a little chuckle when Michael gave the name of the novel he had been prevented from finishing. "I know that novel, yes, I know it well. It is a pity you didn't get to finish it. It has much to say about living life—grasping the golden crown, as they say here in Egypt—living life to its fullest. Taking pleasure completely. Because we never can say what tomorrow can bring. You can be dining at Shepheard's one night and in prison the next day. We both now know that."

Michael lowered his head. He was listening, but he could barely comprehend what Abazar was trying to say. His own life had been too controlled, too limited.

"Do you perchance remember the name of the author of that novel, young Michael?"

"No, I can't remember it. I think I'd know it if I heard it, though."

"Was it perhaps Abazar? Rushdy Abazar?"

Michael thought only a second and responded, "Yes, yes. That was the name I think. Yes I'm sure . . . but, but . . ." he looked up to see Abazar smiling broadly his arms bent, the index fingers of both hands point at his own bulging chest. "That's you? You wrote *The Prince of the Sands?*" Michael's voice was full of awe now.

"Guilty, I must say, and perhaps when I am telling stories—to help us forget where we are—I can remember

46

some of the ending of that novel so that we can make your silly guardian's teeth gnash the next time we meet him. Yes? But for now, eat up. If you finish what's on this plate, we will go over to the cot and sit, side by side, and close our eyes, and I will weave a story for you that will say much of what *The Prince of the Sands* was meant to convey and that will transport us above our present difficulties."

Abazar watched closely, as Michael, his mind already swimming with thoughts that were taking his mind off the present circumstances, ate his food and drank his coffee.

Afterward, they both sat, side by side, on Michael's cot, basking as best they could in the beam of sunlight as it slowly moved up the wall and off their near-naked bodies, and Abazar began to recite a story in a rich, evenly paced baritone. Michael closed his eyes, suddenly feeling his limbs heavy and his mind sinking into a haze in which only Abazar's words were heard, but even they were becoming dim and progressively sounding as if they were coming from an echo chamber at ever-greater distance.

Half way through the story, Abazar put his arm around Michael's shoulder and a hand on the young man's belly—and Michael didn't even open his eyes or flinch.

CHAPTER FOUR: TWIN PRINCES

There once was born to the king of the land beyond the Upper Kingdom twin sons as the first-born of the land. The two boys were perfect and identical in every way at birth, and their mother, the senior wife of Hondo, the war god of the north, the king of the kingdom that buffered the civilized world of the pharaohs from the grasping, primitive world of the beyond, loved the boys equally. Both were perfectly formed boys of marble skin and translucent white hair, which set them apart from all other children of the land beyond the Upper Kingdom. Their mother had been a war offering to Hondo when he had subdued the Hyysoks and had come from the frozen lands of white-haired people beyond the northern sea.

However there cannot be two kings-to-be in a civilized kingdom, and thus the boys were separated from birth, with the first-born by mere minutes, Nebtawi, meaning the lord of the world, being taken into Hondo's court, and the inferior twin, Najja, meaning second born, given over to the senior queen to flourish as he might until such time as

Nebtawi came of age and all possible contenders for the throne were passed into the night.

Now Hondo was jealous of the civilization of the Upper Kingdom and, while he himself spent his reign in the saddle defending his borders from all comers, he decreed that the one who was to rule after him would be learned and wise in the way of governing a people at peace who strove to sophistication and great wealth and comfort.

Thus, at an early age Nebtawi was turned over to the chief eunuch, Bakari, for education and preparation to succeed Hondo, and lived for nineteen years under his close protection. Nebtawi was kept secluded in the black marble palace to protect him from any possible ill intent or any of the diseases that ran rampant in the kingdom. He studied from morning to night, learning to be wise and knowledgeable about finance and military dispositions and, most important, how to balance the needs and intrigues of court, where everyone was scheming for position and a dagger awaited behind every column. Nebtawi grew wise in matter of theory, but not strong nor tested in the ways of real life. His was a delicate disposition, and with each threat of a plague he was rushed to the highest tower of the black marble palace to live in seclusion with his parchments and his teachers until the danger passed. He was permitted no close friends or play companions and had no one permitted to disagree with whatever he said—although by the decree of his father, Bakari's word was law with the young prince.

Hondo dreamed many a plan of passing on his knowledge of kingship to his first born and guiding the lad into his majority, but Hondo's plight was one of continuous warfare to safeguard the borders of the kingdom—and he could never trust the safety of his precious crown prince to the battlefield or its proximity. Thus, with Hondo, the personal interaction with Nebtawi was always something for tomorrow, never for today.

In contrast, Najja, was left to run wild and learn as and what he would. He was raised in the harem, but his mother, the senior queen, was from a sturdy, warfaring peoples herself, and she pushed her son out into the world—when, as he reached the capability, Najja was not dabbling with the women of the harem. The queen knew the custom of the kingdom was that no possible contender for the throne would survive the dying of the previous king, and she decided that Najja would have a life of pleasure and whatever risk and whim aroused him. Eat, drink, make love, go into battle—and be happy, was her philosophy, for tomorrow you die. Nor did she deny Najja his enjoyment with the women of the harem—or the men slaves who served—and he was such a beauty that he never wanted for a companion for a night or an hour.

So, Najja's life was not one of books and theories and antiseptic surroundings. He got down in the dirt with people of the streets and sheep folds and military encampments and learned what he learned by experience and by making mistakes and discovering how to avoid that mistake the next time. He grew strong and tall, and was a presence in the saddle—going into battle on the fringe of his father's guard. He did not ride with Hondo, but he was nearby the king and was able to study his father in battle and in counsel—and he was there in the phalanx of the king's guard whenever danger approached, as it often did.

As years passed, although the people of the kingdom were able to recall—if only barely—that the first-born sons of the Great Hondo were twins, they only saw one. And they came to love this inferior son, Najja, for his contact with the people and his distinctive beauty, observable braveness, and his jovial freedom from care. He was especially appreciated by the young maidens beyond the harem—and some of the young men—of the kingdom for his prowess in a different kind of saddle, and many a by-blow in the kingdom had distinctively blond hair, and more than a handful of the kingdom's minstrels and shepherds could attest to the unequaled sword Najja carried between his strong thighs.

There came a day, shortly after the two young princes had reached their majority, that a great plague was going through the land. The wise crones of the caves advised the people that the surest protection against this scourge was the flesh of the pomegranate, and the trees of the kingdom were soon stripped bare of the life-preserving fruit.

Bakari, secluded with the crown prince Nebtawi in the highest tower of the black marble palace scorned these medieval folk medicines of the crones of the darkness. He peeled over the most modern texts of the day, and thus the prince Nebtawi was bled daily to keep the toxins that would protect his body flowing freely, and Bakari marked it as a favorable sign that the youth's skin took on a more translucent quality with each passing day.

Hondo had listened to his chief counselors and was being bled daily as well. However, he wasn't in the protected environment of the high tower, and while still on the battlefield at the eastern border, he contracted the plague.

He was brought back to the black palace on a bier borne by six virginal sons of the six leading noble families of the realm to the beating of drums in a dirge that Bakari declared would hold off the grasping fingers of death until, through more bleeding, Hondo could regain his strength and throw off the attack of the plague.

At the first news of the king's plight, Najja was seized and removed from the battlefield and returned to the black palace and locked up in the garden of the harem—to await his fate, depending on how Hondo fared.

Such was the consternation in the palace that, as Hondo weakened, all of the senior ministers and generals congregated around his sick bed. This included Bakari, who neglected to lock the crown prince in the high tower when he departed in haste to take his rightful place in the counsel around the sinking body of his king. The prince Nebtawi, of course, was kept as far away from the plague room as possible.

Bored and curious—and now all alone, Bakari never having left him unattended before, Nebtawi descended the stairs of the high tower and wandered through a palace that mostly was completely new territory to him, as sheltered as his life and preparation had been. At length, he came to the gate of a garden enclosed by high stone walls topped with shards of colorful glass. He could see that there were trees and luxurious vines inside the garden—and the key to the gate was in the lock. So, he twisted the key in the lock and pushed on the door. It opened, and he walked into the most lush garden he had ever read about. He had never actually been in one, as Bakari considered plants of any sort as carrying threatening diseases.

His eyes were wide with wonder as he walked down a path bordered by leafy greenery that reached out to him as he passed and beckoned him farther into the center of the world he'd never seen before.

He gasped as he came into the center of the garden, where there was a stone-floored area with burbling fountains at the four points of the compass. In the center of the cleared area was a delicately proportioned tree upon which hung plump, rosy-red fruit.

His gasp, however, was not for the strange and wonderful foliage, but for the young man who sat on a bench under the tree and was nosily devouring fruit from the tree. He had the remains of dripping fruit in each hand and he was happily slurping away, turning from one hand to the other.

He looked up and winked at Nebtawi, and Nebtawi felt his heart leap and other parts of his body stir as well.

The young man was magnificent. He wore only skirts of leather over white cotton and leather sandals with lacings that worked up his calves almost to his knees. He had gold armbands at his bulging biceps, the mark of high rank, so Nebtawi did not shrink from him as he would normally from someone he had just happened upon—although he couldn't remember Bakari ever having permitted that to happen. The young man was heavily muscled and perfectly proportioned. His skin was golden brown, marking him as a man of the open air. But his hair was the whitest of white.

Just like Nebtawi's hair.

Nebtawi was mesmerized by this discovery. He'd never seen a person with hair that was whitest white beyond himself. He had never seen his mother, the senior queen, who did have hair of whitest white, nor, even less, been told that he had any siblings, no less a twin brother.

He was observant enough to realize that this was a mirror image of himself—except a far more robust one than himself. And for the first time in his life, a doubt crept into his being. There was something about this man, something full of life—a life fuller, more robust, more meaningful than his own. But as soon as the thought entered Nebtawi's mind, he dismissed it—or at least pushed it to the side, because it just would not leave his consciousness altogether. There was no one of more privilege and more rewarded in life than he, Nebtawi, was. He was the heir to the Great Hondo. Bakari had constantly told him that all meaning was centered in his, Nebtawi's, life.

"Pomegranate?" Najja asked him with a smile, holding out a half-eaten plump fruit.

Nebtawi shrank away a step. "No. I cannot. It is forbidden. It is unclean."

"It may save your life," Najja said in a jovial voice that took all of the seriousness of the proposition out of the telling. He smiled again broadly. He knew exactly who this was. Najja had not been sheltered from anything. And he enjoyed seeing the delicate, fine-boned young beauty of a man in front of him with skin he could almost see through. But handsome, just like he, Najja, was handsome, both sons having taken after the beauty of the senior queen, who had come to this land as a treasure of regal bearing and awesome beauty.

"It is said to be protection from the plague," he repeated.

"Old crone tale," Nebtawi said haughtily. "Bakari says so."

"Bakari says so, does he?" Najja said with a heartily, not unfriendly laugh. "Suit yourself. Of course, even if it doesn't guard against the plague, it is delicious, and so I will eat of it."

"Who are you?" Nebtawi asked in somewhat halting tones, not quite as sure of himself as he was before.

"Why I am you," Najja roared. "I am you in the world, not in your ebony tower. I am life and fullness . . . and love."

"Love?" Nebtawi asked in a tentative voice. It was obvious he knew nothing of the term.

"Yes. And pain and pleasure—and of pleasure from pain."

"Pleasure from pain?" Nebtawi asked. "There cannot be such a thing. They are opposites. Bakari says so." This was all so confusing to Nebtawi. New and challenging. Nebtawi was not accustomed to be challenged or to be presented with a conundrum that did not have the answer inked at the bottom of the scroll. In Bakari's world there was a logical answer for everything and there was always a white and black and right and wrong.

Still, he was attracted by this new experience—this brash, very familiar man, in a lush garden. All new experiences for Nebtawi. And even more than attracted, Nebtawi was aroused. Of course he didn't know that he was, that this was the name for how tingly and hardening and sensitive his body was beginning to feel. And arousal was something that only increased as Najja stood and loosened his leather skirt and let it fall to the ground—followed by the cotton one—and showed Nebtawi yet one more thing he'd never seen before. A man's sword—in full hardness and curved up toward his belly. Nebtawi saw the swords of men before, and he had one himself, which, as he reached down, he felt was becoming a twin of the other man's. But he'd never seen a sword such as that, not in its fullness. It was a horse's member, not one of man.

"Yes, pleasure can come from pain, just as one such as I can be the same as you. Opposites but just the same." Najja said this with an engaging, mesmerizing smile. "Come I will show you. We are opposites and still the same. And we were born joined and will be joined again now. We can be one, moving as one, and having great pleasure doing so." He was stretching his arms out, hands slicked with the juices of the pomegranates.

And, Nebtawi, in a trance, walked toward Najja, as the more robustly formed of the twins sat back down on the bench and drew his brother onto his lap and demonstrated how pain could grow into pleasure.

Mere days later, the Great King Najja presided over the funeral of his predecessor, Hondo. The counsel was short and without rancor, as being buried with Hondo, to help see him into the other world were many of the court who had joined him in succumbing to the plague—including the great and wise counselor Bakari, and a young prince, Nebtawi, who had been so weak when the plague attacked him that he died in a matter of hours—but whose passing was hardly marked by the people of the kingdom who only knew of—and heartily approved of—the ever-present existence of the accessible, robust, fun-loving, and powerful Prince Najja.

How much more tragic would it have been, though, if the prince Nebtawi had died without ever having lived?

CHAPTER FIVE: INTERLUDE ONE

His story complete, and Michael snoozing in a deep, exhausted sleep in his arms, Abazar ran the tip of a finger around the young man's nipples, first one and then the other. Michael sighed and trembled in Abazar's arms, but he didn't awake. Slowly Abazar ran a hand down the marble-smooth skin of the young man's chest and belly and then on under the waistband of his drawers, raking lightly through the downy hair of his pubes and then cupping his balls and cock. Abazar leaned down and kissed a nipple and then started to tongue down Michael's sternum.

But he stopped, with regret, disengaged, rose, and moved over to his own cot.

It was entirely too easy. No challenge, and he didn't want to take the youth that way. He wanted Michael prepared and open to him.

Later, as Michael was coming out of his deep sleep, he heard cascading water and for a moment thought that he was free and standing near a sylvan waterfall. But he opened his eyes to the same oppressive stone walls.

He was still hearing the water, though, and as he looked to the source of the sound, he sucked in his breath and almost forgot to breathe again.

Abazar was standing in the corner, under the cistern, and was pouring water over his body. He was naked and it was his nakedness that shocked Michael so and made him start almost to hyperventilate. Abazar was hung like a horse. He stopped the flow of the water and soaped his body up. Michael's eyes traced every movement of Abazar's hands as they floated over his curves and crevices and centered between his hips. He was soaping up a cock that was impossibly long and thick and began to engorge and curve up toward his belly as he worked the soap into it with both his hands.

Abazar stood three-quarters to Michael, seemingly oblivious to the young man watching him work his body—seemingly. He had never looked more like a satyr to Michael than now—now that he was naked, and Michael could see that, below the waist, Abazar was almost as heavily pelted as the satyrs in the drawings Michael had seen. And when he turned his head toward Michael and tilted it down and gave the youth a secret little smile, while still working his cock with his hands, Michael felt sensations he'd never felt before.

"I hope you had a good nap—you slept nearly the whole day away," Abazar said, never losing his smile or the grip on his monster cock.

Michael's eyes moved with great difficulty from Abazar's cock to the high window, where he saw that the daylight had, in fact, fled the sky. "I'm sorry. I don't know what made me so sleepy."

"It's the tension. The not knowing, not being in control. It's to be expected. Don't worry about it. Sleep is an escape in our situation. I slept nearly the whole time too."

Abazar had rinsed himself off and was patting his body dry with his linen drawers, after which he put them back on. They clung to him and were almost transparent in their dampness—little use at all in covering anything up. He slowly walked over to Michael's cot and sat down beside him, whereupon Michael popped up in embarrassment and started to wander aimlessly around the cell, hugging himself with tightly embracing arms as if it were cold in the room, although it was closer to sweltering.

"I suggest you clean yourself as well—while there's still enough light to see by. I believe it's important to not let yourself go to spoil, even in situations like this. And I think it will calm you; you seem so keyed up."

"Perhaps later," Michael said with a shaky voice. "Perhaps when it's a bit darker. I'm not used to . . . I've never . . ."

"Don't be afraid of me," Abazar said in his most soothing voice. "We have been thrown together, but I would never want to do you harm—and I will do whatever I can to protect you. I'm sure you will be free soon. I'm sure your family won't let you stay here much longer."

"My family," Michael said bleakly. "I have no family to speak of. And those that I have are like vultures—pecking at me, wanting what I have and doing all they possibly can do to get it. I don't think I'll ever get out of here."

"How can that . . . ? Ah, yes, I see . . ."

"What do you see?"

"Ah, nothing. But you mustn't fret. I'm sure there's someone. That gray suited—"

"Sir Cecil?" Michael burst out with snort. "Yes, I suppose I do represent an investment by him. But someone who cares? No."

"I doubt that. I would say you are a very valuable young man myself. But then, I suppose we are in Cairo, not in America. Why, here in Cairo you would be seen as a Greek god. Here, what you could give would be worth—"

Abazar couldn't be sure Michael was even listening to him now. The young man was pacing and still hugging himself tightly. His voice was reaching a hysterical pitch in what was one of the longest and most revealing of his statements to his cell mate.

"They all look at me with hate and disdain. They want what they think I have, yes, but what do I have? What have I ever—?"

"This is ridiculous," Abazar said, and then, with a voice of authority, as if instructing a child, he continued. "You are coming unglued. That's the last thing that will help you. Come, sit. I will massage your shoulders. You have to do something to calm yourself. I won't bite."

It was the authoritative voice that did it—and Abazar was quick to take note of that. Like an obedient child, Michael came back to the cot and sat down, turning his back to Abazar, who started to work the muscles.

"I feel how tense you are. Tell me about your family, about your life. It will help you relax."

For the next hour, as Abazar rubbed his back in strokes that turned almost into caresses, Michael poured out his woes of being an only child of cold, calculating, ambitious parents, who had been killed in a railroad accident, of his grasping relatives who remained, and of the highly structured, limiting life he'd had—until they were almost in total darkness.

He came back to the reality of how much he was opening to Abazar—much more than he intended—at the sound of the flap in the door opening, and food trays sliding across the floor.

"We eat now," Abazar instructed in the voice of a parent. "Then you clean yourself, while I do some exercises to keep fit—it should be dark enough for you now. And then I will tell you another story. That will soothe you, and I predict you will sleep again like a baby. Tomorrow they will release you. I'm sure. That Sir Cecil sounds like a powerful and resourceful man who will not let you languish here for long."

They started to eat, but Abazar only ate half of his and pulled Michael's away from him half eaten as well.

"I'm not finished," Michael said in surprise.

"Yes you are," Abazar said, the voice of the parent. "We aren't active in here—can't be as active as we normally would be. You need to eat, but you need to regulate yourself too. Go clean yourself now. And I will exercise my body. It would be best if you did so as well."

As Michael rose and moved tentatively over toward the shower and privy corner. Abazar picked up the trays of the half-eaten food, placing Michael's on the floor in front of the food delivery flap in the door and taking his own over and placing it on the floor at a corner of Michael's cot. Then he stood and stretched out his arm and leg muscles and moved to the center of the chamber.

Abazar gave a little grin of amusement, as he saw Michael huddling in the corner, now clothed in darkness, and rinsing and then soaping and then rinsing himself, being careful not to expose himself. At the same time, however, he was surreptitiously watching as Abazar did some sort of dance-like movements in the middle of the cell to stretch and work his muscles—nothing strenuous. But he talked in low, soothing tones as he worked his body, explaining to Michael what each graceful movement did and how it kept his muscles well worked.

Michael watched in fascination but also in increasing embarrassment, as he felt his body tense up and his cock going hard. This shouldn't be happening to him. He had no idea what was happening to him. He just knew that he couldn't stop watching Abazar's graceful, sensuous movements—and that his gathering thoughts about Abazar were ones he should not be having.

He also was growing groggy. There was a ringing in his ears and he felt lightheaded. Not as bad as he had felt after the earlier meal in the day, though. Just in a haze and sluggish.

Abazar had to repeat himself and raise his voice for Michael to hear him. "Come over to the cot now, Michael. I will tell you another story."

Michael walked toward his cot, slightly stumbling, and mumbling to himself. He knew there was something he was forgetting, but the voice of authority had called. And he wanted to hear the story. What he really wanted was the massaging to start again. That had made him melt.

What Michael forgot when he left the shower was to put his drawers back on, so he came to Abazar dazed and naked.

He sat with his back toward Abazar and Abazar started to gently work the youth's back muscles, while in low, mellow tones, quiet enough that Michael had to arch his back toward the storyteller, bringing his ear close to Abazar's lips, to catch it all.

Michael's senses were suspended in some sort of nirvana, where he could hear Abazar's words and where he could feel what Abazar was doing with his hands—and knew that he'd been taught men didn't do this to other men. But that he didn't care, that he was enjoying sensations he'd never felt before and that he was exhilarated in his inner being that it was Abazar who was touching him. That all of his defenses were down.

Thus, when, during the telling of the story, Abazar's hands moved around to Michael's chest and belly, Michael just sighed and leaned back into Abazar's chest. He lay there, murmuring and moaning, and watching his own cock stand straight up and start to throb. Listening to Abazar, getting the gist of what he was saying, absorbing it, as Abazar's hand slowly glided down and wrapped itself around Michael's cock, and stroked him, with Michael's instincts kicking in and his pelvis slowly rolling to the rhythm of the stroking until with a little cry and a sigh, he released his seed, watching it burble up between Abazar's fingers and dribble down his hand.

All the time, Michael was observing, disconnected from his body in all but the sensations of the calming milking, as if this was happening to someone else entirely and he would wake from the trance never having had this experience.

While Abazar continued speaking, spinning his little story out of the air.

CHAPTER SIX: THE SECRET OF THE AURA

Called from his hunt among the mortals below, the minor god Sirith soared into the firmament of the gods on his golden chariot as the wails of grief from the maidens below at the sudden loss of the mighty club they rode in the night screamed up toward him. The coming year would be one of famine and crying in the houses of the Earth-bound wives whose wombs would remain flat and barren no matter how much plowing their husbands gave them—because mere mortals did not understand that when their husbands took them, the golden god Sirith must be taking them too to seed their wombs.

Of all the minor gods of the firmament Sirith was the most handsome, the only one who could have any woman he wanted, goddess or mortal alike. His was a perfectly formed visage, skin white as alabaster marble, his head wreathed in golden-white curls, his lips full and sensuous.

But in his strength was also his weakness.

As he entered in the alternate universe floating above the mortal Earth, everything in mirror image of Earth but manifoldly more magnificent, he heard the hiss and kicked with his heels at Apep, as the snake monster attempted to entwine him and pull him into the world of the in-between. Barely free of Apep, Ammit the destroyer swung his might club at Sirith's head, and it was only the hand of father god Ra, slicing through a beam of light, that stayed Ammit's hand as Sirith rose to the circle of the gods.

"Why did you call me, father god?" Sirith asked as he bowed before the sun disk throne, Ra's consort Hathor at his right hand and the teasing vixen, Bastet, purring at his left. Standing off, and watching the proceedings were Geb, the god of the Earth, Thoth in his wisdom, and Anubis, god of the passing over.

"You have been among the maidens of Earth too long, Sirith. You have lost something, not learned something, and it is sinking you into danger. Did you not feel the bite of Apep and the glancing blow of Ammit's club? You are becoming weak, losing your protection. You must make amends."

"How so, father god Ra? I feel as strong as ever. I can cover Egypt in a night and seed the wombs of countless women. Horus, the pharaoh god, has sung my praises. The banks of the Nile are teeming with new life. The land of the

Egyptians becomes ever stronger, its armies ever larger, from my nocturnal visits."

"Look around you, Sirith. What do you see that the other gods and goddesses have that you do not?"

Sirith looked, but he did not see. He felt Aprep rising through the clouds and wrapping his coils around his ankles. But Sirith kicked free—and he looked harder.

"Is it the brightness?" The gods and goddesses within Sirith's vision did indeed have a presence that he did not. "Is it the aura?" he asked.

"Yes, it is the aura, Sirith," Ra answered. "When you have been too long with Earth, your aura fades. If it were not for the reflection of my light on your golden curls, you would have no more now than a mortal. Your aura is your protection from the world of the in-between and its scavengers, Ammit and Apep. You must regain your aura."

"And how do I do this, father god Ra?" Sirith asked. He was beginning to realize the error of taking his pleasures too long with the mortals of the Earth.

"You must attain the ultimate pleasure, the ultimate love, the ultimate coupling," Ra answered. "Then and only then will your aura shine brightly and protect you."

"I don't understand. I already know the heights of pleasure with the maidens of earth."

"You have no idea of the ultimate coupling, the ultimate pleasure, my son."

"Please then, tell me what I must do."

"The path to ultimate pleasure and the secret of the perpetuating aura lies through earth, wisdom, and death leading to the heat of the sun."

"And that means—?" Sirith started to ask. But when he looked up to the sun throne, Ra and his full retinue were gone.

"It starts with earth, the father god said," Sirith muttered to himself. "And so, back to Earth and a renewal of the nocturnal visitations."

There was great rejoicing and an abundance of expanding wombs when Sirith returned to Earth, but everywhere he went snakes assailed him and monsters flailed at him with their clubs. Clearly this wasn't the answer.

Sirith flew up to the firmament and went straight to his mother goddess, Hathor, who greeted him with a broad smile and open thighs—no goddess being able to deny the plowing golden shaft of the fairest of all the minor gods. But Hathor had no answers for him, only clutching hands trying to hold him fast inside her. Ammit rose into the firmament and chased him to the chambers of Bastet, the cat goddess, purring in her basket of silver weave. Sirith took refuge and sought answers between her trembling thighs, but Apep, who had coiled around the basket raised his head and flicked his fork tongue at Sirith, and Sirith fled back toward the earth.

At the gates of Earth stood Geb, the god of all that was below.

"Earth?" Sirith thought. "Could Ra had meant to start with Geb?"

Geb smiled upon Sirith, having heard his thoughts as clearly as if he had spoken them.

"Yes, it is true. I am the first step to regaining your aura. The first gate is through me."

"Through you? But how so?"

"You must lie with me. You must let me breed you. And then you will be on the first step."

"A god with a god?" Sirith asked in shock. "How can this be?"

"This can be a greater coupling, a greater pleasure, a nearer approach to perpetual aura than lying with any female, Sirith. You only doubt it because you have never experienced it. Gods know no bounds, no limitations. You have limited yourself. And this has weakened you—and faded your aura. Come bend over and spread your legs for me."

Sirith cried out as he was entered for the first time, and then he moved into realms of pleasure he had never experienced before—and felt a slight glow about him after

Geb had moved his staff in and out of his golden channel and buried his seed deep inside the minor god.

"Such is earth," Sirith said when Geb was done with him, "and I see and feel the deepening of the pleasure, the warmer feeling, the glow. But what of the next step, wisdom?"

"You know where to find wisdom, Sirith. And after you have, you will not need to ask such a question again."

Sirith found Thoth, the god of wisdom, who, fortunately, was conferring with Osiris, god of the dead. Apep and Ammit wept with frustration, as Thoth and Osiris gathered Sirith between them and shared his golden channel, thus granting Sirith, highly favored and loved by the gods, two rises in level of understanding and aural protection in one, shared seeding.

Now Sirith didn't have to ask where he needed to go. The father god, Ra, master of the sun, granter of the ultimate understanding, the ultimate pleasure, and the epitome of coupling was sitting on the sun throne, awaiting Sirith, knowing all, knowing Sirith was coming to him. And such was Sirith's blond beauty that even Ra himself was trembling in anticipation of an even higher level of pleasure than he had ever experienced. His powerful staff rose up from between his thighs, Sirith, now having gained the wisdom of what he must do, knelt before the throne and opened his mouth to the staff of Ra.

For forty days and forty nights Sirith gave Ra's staff suck and the heavens opened up to higher levels of understanding and pleasure. And Sirith's aura appeared and expanded. For another forty days and forty nights Sirith's channel rose and fell on Ra's staff as the sun shone ever brighter and Sirith's aura shimmered. Upon the release of Ra's precious seed, a great flood rushed down the Nile, purifying the land of the plague that had beset Egypt in Sirith's absence.

Knowing all now, Sirith realized that there was a balance to be had. In the night he descended on his chariot onto the land of the pharaohs and bestowed his precious seed on the women of Egypt who were ripe for it. But by day, he was in the firmament, at the throne of the father god Ra, rising and falling on the sun god's staff—and experiencing the ultimate of pleasures that he would never have known if he had not grasped life and lived it to the fullest.

And never again was he touched by Apep or Ammit.

CHAPTER SEVEN: INTERLUDE TWO

As Abazar finished the melodious telling of his story, the golden youth, Michael was kneeling between his spread thighs and sucking on the bulb of his cock. Abazar's hands where playing in the curly blond hair of the beautiful youth, and he leaned down and kissed him on the head.

Michael was in a haze still, having heard and absorbed and been moved by Abazar's story, and having some sense of what he was doing—what Abazar had maneuvered him into doing while he was stroking him with the honey-toned telling of his story—but no understanding really of why. He only knew that Abazar's words entered the very center of him and made him ache to live life before he died. He could not forget that he was a prisoner for purposes he knew not, and despite whatever reassuring words Abazar had murmured to him, under no reassurance at all of leaving this cell alive. And he may never have lived before he died. Never have experienced the ultimate of pleasures. And somehow, through the grogginess and the ringing of his ears and fuzziness of his sight, Abazar's story of the ultimate of pleasures—of living—was sinking into his being.

And his body had never reacted before as it was to the suggestiveness of what Abazar was spinning in his stories and to the blossoming of desires and wants—and arousals—that he had never even imagined existed in the barrenness of his prior existence. There had been a flash of insight into that as he was reading into *The Prince of the Sands*, but that had been denied to him. Rushdy Abazar, the creator of that enticing world was here, now. And he was all that was here—and maybe all that Michael would ever know.

Rushdy was offering him the forbidden, while increasingly making him realize that it should not be forbidden. That forbidding it to him was just yet another conditioning cruelty of his parents' world, extended by his grasping uncles and aunts and cousins—and, most of all, by the commanding voice and dictates of Sir Cecil.

But Rushdy had a commanding voice too—the voice of the teacher's authority. And Michael felt that he too long had been the student of death rather than life. Rushdy was promising him life—and pleasure—which was especially sweet as Michael looked into the jaws of death.

Michael had no idea—no recollection—of how or why he had sunk between the hairy knees of the satyr. Only the hazy remembrance of the pleasure and relief that Rushdy had given him and the feeling of obligation—no, of want—to give in return. The voice of authority had told him to kneel, so he had knelt. And the voice of the teacher had instructed him what to do next. And he had done it. And he could feel the pleasure it was giving the storyteller. And thus it was giving him pleasure too.

Rushdy encircled Michael's waist with strong hands and lifted him. He was smiling at Michael, conveying assurances and a promise of new experiences and pleasure. Briefly he hovered the youth's virgin channel over his hardened staff. But then he was speaking to Michael, asking questions, and Michael was just giving sloppy, stupid grins in return.

Abazar could have done it then and there. Finished what he had so carefully started. But the youth wasn't conscious enough. Michael wouldn't be fully ready and willing. The challenge wasn't significant enough yet.

With a sigh of regret, Abazar moved Michael away from him and rose from the cot as he laid the young man down on his back. He leaned over and kissed the youth tenderly on the mouth and then placed his hands on Michael's face and closed his eyelids. Michael almost immediately drifted into the regular breathing of deep sleep, and Abazar was assured that he had been right in holding off.

He wanted Michael to be fully conscious, not in half a haze, and to tell he wanted it, to know he wanted it.

Still, Abazar could not leave him. He was too keyed up. Not the whole way now, certainly—if he could hold off. But part way. Preparation. Preparation for Michael and pleasure for himself. Relief. Partial victory at least. At least that was his reasoning. Because he was smitten, only barely in control of himself. He could not pull away yet. He'd never been so smitten with a conquest. The challenge was what aroused him. The first taking. That's as far as his interest usually went. But with Michael, he wasn't sure. He just wasn't sure.

Abazar sat back down on the cot, beside the thin waist of the golden youth. Michael was laying on his back. Abazar ran the fingers of one hand along Michael's full, sensuous lips, and, with a sigh, Michael opened his lips and two of Abazar's fingers slipped inside. Michael sucked on the fingertips as he had sucked on the bulb of Abazar's cock—almost innocently, certainly unconsciously. Not waking, but stirring a bit. Abazar's eyes were feasting on the vulnerable youth and his other hand was stroking his own cock, bringing it fully back to life again, intent on finishing what he hadn't let Michael finish—hadn't demanded of Michael. A third finger followed the first two.

He gently extracted the moistened fingers from Michael's mouth and lifted the youth's leg on the wall side of the cot and hooked it over his own left shoulder. Abazar leaned over then and scooped his fingers into a large chunk of butter that had been softening on the food tray he had set on the floor at the corner of the cot. He moved his hand to between the youth's now-spread thighs and found and toyed with the entrance of Michael's channel with his heavily greased fingers. Periodically over the next half hour, the hand went back to the tray for more of the butter. He would need plenty of it. Michael moaned in his deep stupor, but still did not awake. Abazar slowly worked the channel with, first, one finger and then two—and four—as slowly, ever so slowly, the tight channel opened to him.

Abazar chuckled at the remembrance of what he had told his cousin, the culture minister—that he would lay Michael on a table of gold and fist his virgin channel in anticipation of a complete taking by his monster cock. Well, there was no golden table in here—just a golden youth. It was not cruelty, though, Abazar reasoned. On the morrow, the young man would have occasion—although he probably never would realize it—to thank Abazar for this preparation. Abazar had a cock that could split a man asunder. And this was a virginal youth.

The fingers were going dry, so Abazar repositioned himself, lowered his face to the precious entrance, and used his tongue to coax the blossoming of the gateway to paradise. Later, when Abazar was breathing heavily and about to come himself, he was able to breach the rim with four knuckles. He would go no further. The groaning Michael—still in a deep sleep but rolling his hips with the movement of Abazar's hand—could not possibly take more, and Abazar was too much on the edge himself. Michael's cock was burbling cum again when Abazar gave a little jerk and found the release he sought.

No more. Not tonight. But tomorrow. If he could just carry Michael a bit further on the pathway to conscious surrender. But to get there, Michael would have to know—to realize—and to appreciate how far they had already come.

Tomorrow was an important day, a very important day. So much had gone into this.

* * * *

"Did you . . . did we . . . last night?"

"No. Why do you ask?"

It was nearly afternoon. Michael had wakened only shortly before and gingerly sat up on his cot, with a groan. Abazar was sitting on his cot, one leg drawn up into his chest, smoking one of the cigarettes that had come on his food tray the previous evening. And staring in Michael's direction.

He could only see Michael as a murky outline through the dust particles in the beam of light coming through the overhead window and lighting up Michael's cot. It was interesting, Abazar had been musing, on how thrown together they were in here but yet how isolated still. It seemed there wasn't far to go. But quite often that last little run to the goal was the hardest. And you could rarely count on it.

The view of Abazar through not just the dust particles but the haze of blue smoke above his head was just as obscured and hazy as was Abazar's view of Michael. The first sensation that Michael had when he woke and sat up was of the face of a handsomely cruel satyr as viewed through a hanging of Spanish lace. It was a confusing sensation to him—fearful and yet exotic and tempting at the same time.

The second sensation was more Earth bound. Not only was his head pounding with a pain that slowly ebbed away as he regained full consciousness, but his insides— particularly his lower channel hurt something murderously.

"Oh, nothing. I just thought that . . . maybe . . . things seemed to be happening. And I don't know if it was in a dream or . . ." He didn't know how to phrase it, and he certainly didn't want to say "My bum burns fiercely." Abazar would laugh at him and say something about the food and his delicate constitution.

"These things . . . these things that seem to be happening, Michael. Do they disturb you?"

A pause and then, "Yes."

"But do they also arouse and entice you?"

No response. Michael found it maddening not to be able to see Abazar's facial expressions clearly through the haze. All he could see was a near-naked body—a magnificently built body, covered with curly hair. And he couldn't truthfully say that wasn't arousing and enticing. The image in his mind went immediately to the monster cock curving up from Abazar's body when he'd seen him under the cascading water. And he shuddered involuntarily.

"Do you understand my stories, Michael? Have you understood the message? It's the same message you would have found in *The Prince of the Sands* if you would have been permitted to read what you wanted to read."

"Yes, I understand . . . I think."

"That's the crux of the matter, Michael. What you have been permitted to do and what has been denied you. You're what, nearly twenty now?"

"Just nineteen. Well, almost nineteen."

"And yet in nearly nineteen years, you haven't lived yet. You are a god among young men in appearance, and you are wealthy beyond all reasonable means. And yet you haven't experienced anything meaningful in life, have you?"

"I wouldn't say that."

"How can you know, Michael? There are so many, many doors you haven't even opened yet. The ultimate pleasure. You haven't even experienced the lower pleasures, have you?"

Silence.

"You haven't even fucked a woman yet, have you?"

Michael was shocked by the sudden rawness of the statement, and he'd squeaked a "no" before he could control his response.

"And yet, as my stories have unfolded for you, there are even greater pleasures to be had. Much beyond this. Do you not understand?"

"I have heard the stories, yes."

"And you have thought on them?"

"Yes."

"And you know that you could have had these thoughts to think if you had been truly free in your life—if your guardian had not controlled what you could and could not do?"

"Yes."

"Life is short, Michael. We know not the hour of our passing."

Silence.

"Do you not believe that, Michael? Here, where you are. In a prison, not knowing your fate—not even knowing why you are here. Knowing only, by your own statements, that there are those who prefer you here, rather than free. And even if not here, under their power rather than free to do as you like, as your instincts call you?"

"Yes . . . yes, I believe that."

The voice was harsh now. "You know the odds are that you will not survive this imprisonment, don't you Michael? That I have been sugarcoating it for you—that most surely I will die for this, but that chances are very good that you will too."

"Yes," the answer came out in gasp as if wrenched from the very center of him, down deeper than the pain in his channel.

"And you will have done so without having lived—because no one has let you live. You will not have been able to experience and experiment with new feelings, instincts that are only now beginning to occur to you."

Silence.

"You have lived more here, in this cell, in the last day and a half than you lived your whole previous nineteen years, haven't you?"

A short pause, and then a strangled, whispered, "Yes."

"And you know you could experience much, much more—more sensation, more pleasure, more meaning—here, now, before it's too late, don't you?"

A resigned, "Yes."

"Come to me. Come over here to me, Michael." The voice was melodious, deep, but it had a rod of steel running through it.

Silence for a few moments and then a sobbed, "I can't. I don't think I can. I'm scared."

"You won't maybe. Not just this moment. But you can, Michael. I think you can. I think you understand you must. That you understand you want to live before you die. You say you can't come here. What if I come to you?"

The tension in the chamber was shattered by the sound of the grating of the bolt on the food door and the scraping of two food trays along the follow.

Flustered, Michael stood, ready to escape from the enticing trap that was entangling him, seeking anything to move this on to surer ground.

"No, leave it," Abazar commanded, and Michael's movement was arrested even as he was rising from the cot. "You indicate that the food may be adversely affecting you. Leave it for now."

Michael sank back down onto the cot, but Abazar rose and walked through the beam of dust, becoming more palpable—more arousing—to Michael with each step and causing Michael to breath heavily. Abazar walked to the door and leaned down and picked up the black lacquer tray— always the black lacquer tray, never the red one—and set it down on the table, sank to the stool, and ate and drank heavily.

As had been the case for the last couple of meals, each tray had an inordinately large chunk of butter on the side. Abazar didn't use this. He pushed the butter to the side of the tray. And when he was finished, he went to the door and picked up the other tray and placed it on the table as well. Using his fingers, he transferred the butter chunk from the tray that still had food on to it to the other tray, plopping it on top of the butter that was already there. He turned then and looked at Michael, smiled, and said. "And would you like another story now?"

"Yes," Michael answered quickly, before looking surprised at himself for doing so.

"And I shall come there to your cot to tell you this story, shall I?"

A pause, but then a murmur of assent.

Abazar picked up the tray from which the food had been eaten and on which only a double chunk of butter now lay, walked slowly over to Michael's cot, laid the tray on the floor at the corner of the cot, and stood there, smiling down at Michael for a moment before stripping off his drawers.

Michael gasped and drew in his breath. Abazar's cock was at half erection.

"Will you take yours off, or shall I do it for you?"

Michael reached for the waistband of his drawers with hands trembling from an anticipation that was arousing, but he was fumbling, and Abazar gave a little laugh and reached down and drew them down and off Michael's legs himself. Then he came down onto the cot behind Michael and drew Michael's legs up onto the cot so that he lay, his back to Abazar's front, stretched out on the cot.

"And so we begin. A shorter story, I believe." As he whispered this into Michael's ear, he leaned over him and his fingers went to the chunk of butter on tray on the floor at the corner of the cot.

CHAPTER EIGHT: GREENER PASTURES

The mare had everything she could want. There was no beauty greater than she was. She had a rich, milky white coat and golden mane and tail and, although not large of stature, she was perfectly proportioned. She had been raised from a foal in the King of Persia's private circus and was never taxed with anything more strenuous than riding around the ring with a dwarf on her back—a contrasting of beauty and the beast—when the King of Persia chose to entertain with his private circus, which was not often.

When not called to the palace ring, especially built for the elite circus troupe to perform in, the mare was pampered and groomed twice daily and permitted to roam as she pleased within the confines of a small enclosure at the fringe of the king's summer palace in Esfahan.

Beyond the walls of the enclosure toward the west stretched the plains, with the snow-capped Zagros mountains in the distance. Toward the east the land went on forever beyond a low ridge in the foreground—and the mare looked toward that direction with the feeling of freedom to roam.

The mare was given the choicest of delicacies and slept in a warm barn every night. She had three keepers who loved her dearly and attended her every move, ensuring that she was safe from all harm.

Everyone thought that the mare could not be happier, could not be more content. They felt her tremble to their touch and heard her sighing whinny when they groomed her—and they attributed that to pleasure and contentment. The path of mud that circled her small enclosure close to the walls to the outside world they attributed to her devotion to exercise, and they were happy to clean her hooves carefully each evening as they led her into her solitary barn and guided her muzzle into a trough containing food fit for a queen.

And that's how they thought of her. A privileged queen, kept immaculately beautiful, shown off for short periods at the whim of the King of Persia, and protected from all the evil and cruelties of the outside world.

It was in the spring, as the snows were receding along the ground back to the base of the Zagros peaks that the mare first saw him. The first time, in the dawning of the day, racing, free and majestically across the ridge to the east, highlighted by the red-orange-yellow of the rising sun.

The mare stopped in her tracks, mesmerized by the size of him and the dancing lope of his gait. He was jet black, curly black hair everywhere. And he was strong and arrogant and something unlike anything the mare had seen before.

And most of all he was free. And he was male. Sensuous and arousing in a way the mare had never felt before.

She could not help looking to the east every morning she was let out in her small enclosures. Some days he was there. Some days he was not.

The black stallion took her breath away. Not just because of his magnificence, but also because he was free and was racing across the plain as he would.

At first she withdrew from the wall, not wanting him to know she was there. But increasingly she became bolder and bolder. And he did notice she was there—long before she realized he did.

He looked at the life she led and he did not see privilege and safety and contentment. He saw something else. He saw that she was not free. And he also saw that she was beautiful. And his juices flowed and he wanted her.

No one could explain how the tiers of logs of the wall of the mare's enclosure's eastern wall came down early one morning. The mare certainly wasn't strong enough to have done this. And why would she anyway? She had all she needed inside the enclosure. Nearly every mare across the empire wanted what she had and would trade positions with her in a moment.

But the reality was that she was not there on the morning the wall came down. Nor was she anywhere nearby.

She was out on the plain, at first running free and wild and at length running in front of the magnificent black stallion—not knowing even herself if she were running from him in fear of the unknown or running *for* him, teasing and enticing him.

But the stallion let her run, staying ever close to her, giving her her freedom to run, knowing that she would tire and present herself to him—because he knew it was what she wanted, a greater freedom, an ultimate pleasure.

And so, she did. High at the peak of a ridge just short of the foothills of the snow-capped Zagros Mountains, the mare stopped, breathing heavily, seeing that her breath came out of her nostrils in clouds of joy—the joy of running free and being prepared for the ultimate pleasure.

She presented herself, spreading and setting her legs and lifting her tail. With a loud snort of victory, the black stallion mounted her.

She shuddered and trembled and whinnied in the pain-pleasure of her first glorious taking, as he entered her strongly and deeply, stronger and more deeply than she could ever have imagined.

And thrust.

And thrust.

And thrust, flooding her deeply with the seeding of the ultimate pleasure.

CHAPTER NINE: THE ULTIMATE PLEASURE

Michael cried out in pain-pleasure each time Abazar cried out the word "thrust" as he concluded the story. And each thrust in the story was matched by a thrust of Abazar's cock inside the rim of Michael's channel. Despite the butter and the preparation the evening before, Abazar's thrusts, though they made Michael feel he was being jammed with a tree trunk, took him not much further in than the sheathing of his bulbous cock head. Part of it was the position and the angle. He was stretched behind Michael and holding the young man's leg up to give himself purchase, and, on the small cot, this would have made "to-the-hilt" work difficult. But it was also Michael. He had been too tense. He had cried out too pleadingly—even though he had demurred when Abazar had offered to give him rest—but he had just gone too rigid.

So, when Abazar brought his story to a close, intending that the seeding of the mare would be the high point of his ejaculation as well, he was only rewarded with a spouting from Michael.

Michael was panting and moaning, and he was wracked with sobbing between the moans, although he tried to muffle it, assuring Abazar that he wanted what Abazar was providing. Abazar held him in a tight embrace and then kissed him on the neck and began to glide his free hand over the trembling marble-white skin of the young man.

"I'm sorry," Michael murmured.

"Sorry?" Abazar whispered back. "The first time is often so. You must not be so tense. But it was good."

"But you have not come, have you?" Michael asked. His voice was unsure. He couldn't really tell one way or other—he just felt that it hadn't been all that Abazar had sought.

"I am not wholly satisfied, no," Abazar said in a low voice. He saw no reason to lie. "But that means that a deeper experience is only moments away."

Michael stopped breathing and tensed up. "Again? So soon?" he asked, in voice tremulous.

"And again and again and again," Abazar. "Until they come to take us away. My story. You were listening to my story? I am the black stallion—that's, in truth, an image they have for me in the bazaar—no doubt gleaned from the men I have known. They call me the Stallion of Heliopolis. And you are the milk-white mare. This is not an ending; this is a beginning. I will ride you. I will fuck you until the cum flows from your eye sockets and your ears. I will—" He stopped, however, as he sensed from the tensing of Michael that it was not time for such talk yet.

"Please . . . Rushdy . . . I don't know if I can—"

"What are you afraid of, little one? This is only a slitting of the door. This is an opening to a whole new world for you. Why are you so tense?"

"I don't know if this is me, Rushdy. It's a sin. I should be fighting it—I am wanting it, seeking it. I can't . . ."

Abazar's spirits sank. This was exactly the point. The crux of the challenge for him. The young man must want it, must seek it. Otherwise it wasn't complete for Abazar; it wasn't the ultimate pleasure for him.

"You are just virginal," he whispered. "And alas, I am a stallion. I know when you have all of me inside you, me riding you in glorious rhythm, all of your fears and inhibitions will evaporate. As soon as you experience the ultimate pleasure."

The tension inside Michael wasn't lessening; if anything it was stiffening. Abazar had to think of something. It was all for naught if the young man wouldn't beg for it— and receive the fullness of it. His eyes traveled around the room, searching for some idea of what to do. He could just

95

turn the golden youth to a position where he could mount him fully and just take him and plow him until Michael completely surrendered. But what if that didn't work? He had invested too much in this challenge to not have his victory.

His eyes went to the walls across the chamber from the cot, and he smiled.

"What if you had no control, if you welcomed it and wanted it and had no control, no way to stop it?" he asked.

"Hasn't that been my life so far?" Michael asked wearily. "Not having control."

"Yes, it is the problem, but it may also be the gateway to the solution. You have not had control before—but you were being forced to do things you did not want to do. What if, at least for a beginning, you had no control but you were being given what you want. That could help get you past the block in your pleasure and your being able to receive it fully."

Michael said nothing, mulling over this conundrum. His thoughts went back to the small reception room at Shepheard's, to the Nubian taking the waiter. He had been aroused by that then—and even more so in thinking upon it since. And he knew now that part of the arousal was that the waiter had no choice, no control. And when Michael thought of the Nubian coming to him after finishing with the waiter, the arousal he felt was couched in being taken by force, without his consent, beyond his control.

"We have come so far. You do want the ultimate lovemaking, don't you? You do want the feel and to have the knowledge of every inch of me inside you, don't you? The joy of knowing you are being so fully possessed and that you have the effect on me to keep me hard and having my seed flowing deep inside you? Knowing that tomorrow we might both be dead?"

"Yes," the answer was breathy, as while Rushdy talked, he was slowly stroking Michael's cock again, and the youth was responding to the arousal.

Michael turned his head and looked into Rushdy's eyes, only to see that Rushdy was staring away from him. He followed the satyr's line of sight and shuddered and moaned when he saw what Rushdy's attention was focused on.

Abazar had moved the table aside, and he used his and Michael's linen drawers to wrap the youth's wrists in so that the manacles hanging from two adjacent iron rings on the wall didn't chaff his skin too badly.

Michael was barely able to reach the floor with the balls of his feet when he hung from the manacles on the wall, but that didn't matter for very long, as Abazar moved in close to Michael and reached down and cupped and spread his buttocks in strong hands as Michael raised his legs on Abazar's hips.

The first entry in this position was arduous, but Abazar assured Michael that it would open him as the position on the cot had not.

Michael cried out as the bulb of Abazar's cock breached the rim of his channel, and panted and whined that maybe they should leave it for later.

"You are my prisoner now; you will be fucked deeply before I unshackle you," Abazar growled, which caused Michael to look into his eyes with fear. But all he saw was an encouraging smile. "It's what you want, isn't it? No control over the inevitable. No responsibility. I take all responsibility."

"Yes," Michael murmured. "It's what I want." And then "Oh, my God!" he was crying out, as Abazar's cock gained a good two inches of depth never reached before. Visions of the Nubian taking the waiter flowed through Michael's mind and he felt his channel slackening and his captor moving, gliding deeper inside him. And Michael wanted it all. He wanted Rushdy inside him, and he wanted the Nubian inside him. He wanted to experience, to live it all. All Egyptian men, the men of the world. He wanted them all inside him. His channel relaxed, the muscles of his channel walls beginning to work with the shaft that was splitting him.

Michael rode Abazar's hips with his legs and arched his back and shuddered and writhed as Abazar's staff reached the depth of a normal man's cock in his well-buttered channel.

"You've done it, golden one," Abazar whispered in his ear. "This is the best that most men could do. I could work you here—and you would enjoy it. It is not ultimate, though. Do you want the ultimate?"

"Yes, oh yes," Michael whispered through his groaning.

Abazar pressed in another inch and held there for several moments, both of them breathing heavily. He dipped his face to Michael's and they kissed deeply, and Abazar then let his tongue run down along the side of Michael's throat and down to his nipples. He waited until Michael stopped trembling. The youth was moaning, hanging from the rings, control of his arms completely taken away from him.

Michael could feel Abazar trembling now. Abazar took Michael's calves in his hands and leaned in and kissed him on the lips again. Michael was whimpering, knowing he was at the moment—the gateway to the ultimate.

"Forgive me, little one," Abazar murmured. "Just a few seconds. Only a few seconds. And then, slowly but surely, the journey to paradise."

Michael was already opening his mouth to scream out when Abazar jerked his legs wide and thrust hard inside his channel with his cock. Michael cried out and writhed and pleaded, but saddled to the hilt now and having faith that Abazar wasn't lying to him and that the pleasure would progressively overcome the pain, he gave all control, all tension, up to the command of this satyr who now fully possessed him. Feeling the full surrender, Abazar gave a snort of victory and completion and began to pump in short, sure strokes deep inside his conquest until they both felt the flow of him deep inside Michael's no-longer-virginal channel.

It had been good for both of them—but not the ultimate, at least for Abazar. And suddenly, as never before, it was important to Abazar that it be everything with Michael. He couldn't see himself subjugating, deflowering, and then leaving Michael as he had done with so many other young men he had pursued and conquered.

Michael was still whimpering and quietly sobbing when Abazar released him from the manacles. Abazar kicked the table back into place—and a stool—and laid Michael gingerly down on his back on the table.

He spread Michael's legs and took him again, more slowly, more rhythmically, making sure that Michael could now accommodate him without tensing up. And with all surrendered now, Michael relaxed and took Abazar at great depth now, and his moanings now were ones of ecstasy and fulfillment rather than fear and pain.

Finished, Abazar leaned into Michael and kissed him on the lips. Then he picked him up in his arms and settled him on the stool at the table.

"You were magnificent," he murmured, to assure the youth, even though it still had not been complete for him—it had all been what he did, not what Michael begged for. It had been good enough, he knew, for Michael to accept it as ultimate. "Now. Now, you may eat your dinner. All of it. It will help you rest."

And then Abazar sat close to Michael on the other stool, an arm around the youth's shoulder, running his fingers over Michael's naked body as the lad ate from the red lacquer tray. He didn't eat it all, only about half, but his eyelids were heavy with an overarching tiredness and his aching limbs were numbing when Abazar picked him up in his arms and moved across the chamber and laid him out, lovingly on his cot.

It was nearly dawn when Abazar received the ultimate pleasure he was seeking. He woke to the warmth of Michael's lips closing over the bulb of his cock. And later, when they were both breathing heavy and in highest heat, Michael glided up to lie full length beside him. They lay there for a few minutes, and Michael began to move his hands around on Abazar's body, playing in the matting of hair. The hand kept going back to Abazar's cock.

Abazar's spirits were soaring. Michael was offering himself, wanted what Abazar could give him. His actions were making this clear. His was so close to the ultimate pleasure he strove for, but the youth had to take that last step.

"You want fucking?" he murmured in the dark.

"Yes," Michael whispered. "I want you inside me again."

"If you want it, you must take it."

He could feel the intake of Michael's breath. "How? I don't—"

"You have to fuck yourself on me." Abazar reclined fully on his back, his monster cock reaching for the ceiling of the chamber and with gratitude and a feeling of total victory watched in the gathering light Michael start to mount his hips.

But that wasn't enough, even that. Abazar raised his strong arms and held Michael there, hovering over him.

Michael was groaning, wanting it.

"Beg. Plead. Declare your need."

"Please, Rushdy, please. I want it, please. Please fuck me."

Abazar gave a deep-throated laugh of triumph and settled Michael over his pelvis. With great effort and much groaning, Michael swallowed Abazar's cock with his channel.

And when he was fully sheathed, he began to move as a camel across the endless sand dunes.

After a wild and satisfying ride ending in mutual fountaining, Abazar commanded Michael to leave his cot and eat the rest of the food that had been left on the red lacquer tray, and then the young man entered a deep sleep on his own cot.

The conquest was complete. Michael had come for it, willingly, on his own. And he had taken it joyously, with no reservations.

CHAPTER TEN: THE UNFOLDING

When Michael woke this time, he was lying naked, between silken sheets in a canopied bed in the center of a large, stonewalled room, bathed in sunshine from three French doors out onto a stone balcony and richly appointed with an Oriental carpet, brocade-upholstered chairs, gilded chandelier, and heavy damask draperies on windows and bed.

"Ah, so prince charming awakens once more."

Rushdy Abazar was standing in the open door to the hallway. He was leaning up against the frame of the door, wearing a silken white robe that hung open, revealing he was naked underneath. His cock looked very much like it was ready for action.

"Where are we?"

"I just had us moved upstairs. I thought we might be a little more comfortable here."

"Then it was all a ruse," Michael said in a flat voice.

"Much of it was, yes. I didn't really lie. Early on I said I lived in Heliopolis and could see the minaret from the windows of my home. I just didn't say that the window you were looking from was one of the windows of my home. But not all ruse, no. Not the part of you responding fully to the lovemaking, certainly. You did so—eventually—you know. Do you regret that?"

A short silence, but then a reluctant "No. But it was all just an elaborate scheme to get me in bed? You didn't really write *The Prince of the Sands?*"

"Oh, yes, I wrote it—and I think you needed to absorb every bit of what I wrote in it. Yes it was a scheme with one goal. I think you were worth it. Don't you . . . now?"

"Yes, I guess so."

"And do you really think you have responded in any other way than you secretly wanted to do."

"No, I guess not."

"Good. I'd hate to think we'd be retrogressing. There was nothing ruse about what I told you about the ultimate pleasure or your needing to find a life of your own, was there?"

"No. I'm beyond that, thanks. But my groggy periods and long sleeps and all—?"

"Sorry about the groggy periods. Drugged food, you know. Although I assumed you'd figure that out soon enough. And most of it was for your own good. The trauma of captivity and all. It kept you calmer."

"And it helped get your cock inside me," Michael said with a sharp tone.

"Ah, see. Already you are liberated in your talk of what is a natural, very enjoyable act. Two days ago I don't think your handlers would have allowed you to even say the word 'cock.'"

"No doubt you're right."

"And I've liberated you of that."

"Yes you have."

"And you resent that?"

"No, not particularly."

"Good. Because I don't think you have forgotten last night—when you came to me and begged for the cocking. You weren't drugged then. I didn't let you have the drugged food, did I? I let you decide entirely on your own."

"Yes. That's right. I won't deny it."

"And when I offer you a good cocking now, you'll take it? You'll want it? You'll even beg for it if I hold it back from you?"

"Yes, yes, of course." It came out on a long sigh of resignation.

"You asked if it was all a ruse. But, no, I actually saved you from captivity. I did scheme to kidnap you for myself, yes, but my men actually saved you from a kidnapping. Can you imagine that? My men said they weren't the ones who first tried to spirit you away in the courtyard at Shepheard's."

"It matches what I was feeling at the time, yes."

"So, you are a very popular young man."

"Apparently so, yes."

"And I can readily understand why," Abazar said. "You are a very desirable young man. So much so that I don't know if I can let you go—just yet. Oh, I'll let you reunite with your guardian—although I would suggest you start showing some backbone in that department—and you can proceed on your Nile adventure, just a few days later than planned. But, once again, when I drop this robe and come over to that bed, will you deny me?"

"No." It was said in a small, but determined voice.

"You want the cock? Now? Of all that has transpired, that's the one thing you know you want—of your own free will?"

"Yes." The answer was breathy. Michael moved to the foot of the bed, lying on his back, and opened his thighs to Abazar.

Abazar smiled and started to shrug the robe off his shoulders, but just then a servant appeared at the other end of the hall.

"Effendi," he said. "I am sorry to disturb you, but there are some gentlemen downstairs who—"

"Tell them to come back some other time. Tell them—"

"They are policemen, Effendi. And they say if you won't come down, they'll come up."

"Oh very well, then," Abazar responded almost listlessly, as if this was a small irritant.

Before he left, he turned to Michael and said, "I won't be long. Stay where you are, please."

This may have been a mistake.

As he feared, When he descended the stairs, he found, standing impatiently in his foyer both the chief of Cairo's police, Raymond Little, and Michael's guardian and solicitor, Sir Cecil Pills. There also was a bevy of Egyptian policemen in blue uniforms, including the Nubian Abazar had seen guarding Little in the Gentlemen's Dining Room at Shepheard's. At a signal from Little, the policeman fanned out, with several, led by the Nubian ascending the staircase.

"You needn't deny you are holding Sir Cecil's ward here, Rushdy," Little said.

"Nor will I deny it," Abazar answered haughtily. "I was saving the young gentleman from harm. He was being kidnapped outside of Shepheard's when my men rescued him. You wouldn't already know anything about that, would you, Little?"

"I might," Little answered without apology. "I'm afraid that Ismail Wazzier Bey is a bit displeased that his playmate did not appear that evening. He found other amusement."

Abazar blanched a bit at the name of the regional governor, a notorious raper of young men—even more active and much more cruel than he was himself. He had assumed Little had intended Michael for himself. It was more sensitive that it went higher than that—if, of course, Little wasn't lying.

"So that little assault tableau Michael told me about in the locked reception room at Shepheard's? That was all staged to force Michael out into the night and into the arms of the bey's men?"

"Yes. The waiter was my sergeant's reward for delivering young Powell. He would have pushed Powell out into the courtyard if he hadn't left before the sergeant was finished with the waiter. And you disrupted that. You will have to pay extra, I'm afraid, if you wish to keep the young gentleman and make restitution to the bey—not to mention cover my lost arrangement fees."

"I'm good for any cost required," Abazar responded. "You know that, of course, or you would not have approached through my front door. And you, Sir Cecil," he continued, turning on the British solicitor. "You countenance all of this? Michael is your ward, and not just any street urchin to be bought and sold for anyone's pleasure. What is this to you?"

"I am the solicitor of several of his relatives in America as well," Sir Cecil said. "I need a new roof on my London house." He shrugged and would have said no more, if Abazar hadn't pressed him.

"And Michael? What am I to do with Michael when I have grown tired of him?"

"It would be best, of course—for all of us—if Michael never stepped foot out of this house again."

"Ah. And what of his inheritance? Would I perhaps—?"

"It is untouchable for nearly seven years—until Michael would have become twenty-five. The conditions are iron clad, although in Michael's absence, his relatives—with my help—may be able to dislodge some of it. Michael gone then, what is left, in time, will be distributed among his living relatives. I, of course receive a yearly fee for administering the estate. But there's no money until he reaches twenty-five . . . it would be out of the question—"

"And there's still a possibility of unpleasantness over the disappearance of the young man," Little interjected, "and just who might have committed what crime."

"In which case, your management fee wouldn't amount to much, would it, Raymond?" Abazar said with a voice that was smooth as silk and that, he hoped, covered how fast his mind was working to stay on top of this cat-and-mouse negotiation. "Or perhaps you, Sir Cecil, would be covering that from the yearly fee you work so hard to earn?"

"Not likely," Sir Cecil said dryly. "If arrangements cannot be made here, it is still a long, dangerous trip up the Nile. Leaving Michael in your hands is just a tidy convenience in my perspective."

"Then, be it so, gentlemen. I think you can see yourselves out. I have business to finish upstairs. And do take your minions with you, please."

As Abazar turned and mounted the stairs, as slowly and deliberately as he could manage despite the knocking of his knees on how close a thing that had been for him—and for Michael, Little blew on a whistle and Egyptian men in blue started to reappear out of the woodwork and shuttled out of the main door to the palace.

Abazar knew what he had to do. It would be simple, but as far as he figured, it would be effective. He had known before even now that Michael was worth too much to let go—at least for now. They would have nearly seven years, during which Abazar would mentor Michael as Sir Cecil never had. And then Michael could reappear in Boston—to the utter consternation of his relatives—and claim his fortune and whatever new life he wanted.

When Abazar reached the door to his bed chamber, he was stopped dead in his tracks in horror mixed with arousal.

Michael was still on his back near the foot of the bed. The Nubian was standing between his spread legs and grasping Michael's ankles in his fists as he plowed Michael deep.

Abazar watched in stunned fascination, aroused as well as outraged, his eyes focused on the bulbous butt cheeks of the heavily muscled Nubian watching them contract and expand, push forward and retract—with Michael, grasping the man's waist and moving with him—meeting his deep thrusts with counterthrusts of his own, moaning softly. Abazar looked into Michael's face—into his hooded eyes and slightly open mouth with its lopsided grin, and saw that the young man was thoroughly enjoying the fucking. Michael arched his back and gave a little yelp of pleasure and reached for the Nubian's buttocks, digging his fingernails into the black flesh as the Nubian's staff achieved greater depth.

"Michael, you've come a long way," Abazar muttered in half amused, half speculative amazement.

"It was my sergeant who found that the young man was here. I promised him his reward. If you had not agreed to deal with the young man, the sergeant would have been quite pleased to do so." The statement came from Raymond Little, who had followed Abazar up the stairs and was standing beside him at the doorway.

Both watched, their hands going to their crotches, neither giving any thought to intervening, because both the Nubian and Michael were well into the ultimate pleasure, the Nubian beginning to establish a long deep rhythm and Michael groaning, spreading his legs as far apart as he could to receive every inch of the monster cock, and moving his pelvis in harmony with the fuck.

"And what of Sir Cecil?" Abazar said in a low voice. "How much extra for him to have an unfortunate accident on the Nile?"

"Not much," answered Little. "I don't like him much. An Englishman would have to be crazy to come to Cairo at a time like now anyway."

ABOUT THE AUTHOR

HABU is one of the pen names of a former supersonic spy jet pilot, intelligence agent, male model, movie actor, and diplomat. An American, he is a published mainstream novelist and short story writer under another name and in another dimension of his life, but he has written or cowritten (with Sabb) over 500 published short stories and numerous published erotica e-books, primarily of gay fiction but also memoir, straight fiction and ménage fiction. His hand and creative writing can be seen in stories and books by habu, sr71plt, shabbu, and Stephen Kessel—among unrevealed others that might surprise readers. The fictionalized GM memoir *Flying High* is loosely based on his life experiences.

Barbarian Spy

for Literary Heat

BOOKS BY HABU
The Indian Prince
The Handyman
Grab Bag
Cairo Surrender
Fetish Galore!
Homeward Bound
Journey to Mirage
Choke Hold
Sporting Life
BOOKS BY SHABBU
Dirty Pool
Operation Black Jade

Yap, Yap
Cigars!
Angel in the Barn
Gayly Complicated
Despoiling David
The Tree of Idleness
Rough Road to Happiness
I Met a Man
The Interview
Rough Road to Happiness